G.A. Henty

Dorothy's Double
Volume 3

G.A. Henty

Dorothy's Double
Volume 3

1st Edition | ISBN: 978-3-75238-271-6

Place of Publication: Frankfurt am Main, Germany

Year of Publication: 2020

Outlook Verlag GmbH, Germany.

Reproduction of the original.

DOROTHY'S DOUBLE
BY G. A. HENTY
VOL. III.

CHAPTER XVII

Higher and higher rose the flames as fresh sticks were constantly piled on. The blood again began to circulate through the veins, and enjoyable as the heat was, the sharp tingling in the hands and feet caused the girls acute pain. Then came a feeling of pleasant drowsiness.

'It will do them no harm to go to sleep, I suppose?' Mr. Hawtrey asked Giuseppe.

'No, monsieur. Now that they are warm it is the best thing for them. We will keep up the fire.'

Scarcely a word had yet been spoken. Both Mr. Hawtrey and his friend were completely exhausted. Since they had left the glacier they had staggered along in a half-stupefied condition, feeling that in spite of their exertions they were gradually becoming more and more chilled. As soon as the fire blazed up and there was nothing more to do for the girls, they had thrown themselves down near the fire, and a feeling of drowsiness, against which they had been fighting ever since the storm struck them, was now almost overpowering. Giuseppe produced from his wallet a bottle of wine and some cold meat and bread. These had formed part of the supply that had been brought up for lunch. The rest had been left behind, at the spot where they had started on the glacier.

'Let us eat, monsieur,' he said to Captain Armstrong.

'But the others will want something when they wake.'

'Conrad will start as soon as he has eaten, monsieur, to get help. It is two o'clock now; he will be down at the village in three hours, and will bring up porters and food. The ladies will not be able to walk. It has been a narrow escape.'

'It has indeed. We all owe our lives to you, my good fellows.'

'It is our business,' the man said simply; 'we were wrong in letting you go on to the glacier, but we did not think the storm would have come on so quickly. Sometimes the clouds will be like that for hours before they burst; but it is getting late in the season, and we ought to have run no risks.'

Just as they had finished their meal Giuseppe exclaimed, 'I hear a shout!'

The others listened, and above the roaring of the wind in the pines overhead they heard the sharp bark of a dog.

'It must be a rescue party,' Conrad said, leaping to his feet. 'They are sure to have seen the clouds rolling down the mountains, and would know that there was a storm raging up here,' and accompanied by Giuseppe he hurried away in the direction from which the sound had come, shouting occasionally as they went.

In five minutes Captain Armstrong heard them returning, and the sound of voices and of stumbling feet among the rocks showed that they had a party with them. He rose to his feet just as the figures of the guides, with three or four men, emerged from the mist.

'Thank God we have found you, Armstrong!' Lord Halliburn said, grasping his hand. 'We have had a terrible fright about you all. It was somewhere about eleven when one of the guides ran up to the hotel saying that there was a storm raging amongst the hills, that the clouds had swept across the Mer de Glace, and he was certain the party that had gone up this morning must have been overtaken by it. You may imagine that we lost no time. The guides knew what to do, and got together twenty men, with stretchers and ropes; then we got a lot of blankets from the hotel, and brandy, cold soup, and things of that sort, and started. Till we were more than half way up we were inclined to believe that the fears of the guides were exaggerated, for although we could see the clouds flying fast overhead there was not a breath of wind. However, for the last hour we have had a desperate fight for it. Though we had brought wraps with us, the wind and driving snow were terrible, and we began to despair of ever seeing any of you alive again. We were almost as surprised as delighted when your guides met us and assured me that you were all safe. Where are the others?'

'There they are, sound asleep. The heat of the fire after the bitter cold sent them off at once.'

'Do not disturb them till we have heated some soup and got some boiling water ready,' Giuseppe said. 'Some hot soup for the ladies, and some of the same with some hot spirits and water for the men, will do wonders for them.'

A few minutes later Mr. Hawtrey was roused. He looked round in bewilderment at the men clustered on the other side of the fire.

'Thank you and your friends most heartily, Halliburn, for hurrying so promptly to our rescue,' he said, as soon as he understood the situation. 'One of the guides told me when we got here that he was going to start for help, but that would have meant six or seven hours' delay, and the sooner the girls are in bed the better for them.'

Mr. Fortescue was next aroused, and then he and Mr. Hawtrey woke the girls. They, however, were unable to rise to their feet, their limbs being completely stiffened by cold and fatigue. A basin of hot soup with bread broken into it restored them wonderfully.

'How are we to get down, father?' Dorothy asked.

'You will be carried, dear; the men have brought up stretchers and plenty of blankets and wraps, and there are mules for Fortescue and myself half a mile lower. We can manage to get as far as that, though I feel as if I had been beaten almost into a jelly. It is Lord Halliburn and his friends who have brought this party to our rescue, dear,' for the men had, at the suggestion of the guide, all retired a short distance from the fire when the girls were awakened, as he said that it was better that they should not be confused by seeing themselves surrounded by strange faces.

'It is very good of them,' Dorothy said. 'I was wondering vaguely while I was taking the soup where it had come from, and could not make out what you meant by the stretchers and mules, because I remember we sent those that we came up on, back to the hotel. Where is Lord Halliburn?'

'Halliburn, will you and your friends show yourselves,' Mr. Hawtrey said. 'The ladies are now ready to receive company.'

There was but a short chat, then the stretchers were brought up and the girls helped to take their places upon them. They were then covered up closely with blankets. The porters lifted them, and the party started down the hill, the older men being assisted by a porter on each side, for they were scarcely able to drag themselves along. Being urged by Mr. Hawtrey to go on at once, the rescue party and Captain Armstrong pushed forward at the top of their speed. Being now well wrapped up they felt the cold but little, and in half an hour reached the spot where the mules were awaiting them, and then proceeded quietly down the hill, the porters with the ladies being already far ahead.

On the way down Captain Armstrong related the incidents of their adventure.

'It was touch and go,' he said. 'Another quarter of an hour on that glacier would, I believe, have finished us all. It was not fatigue so much as it was the loss of heart that one felt. The wind seemed to go right through one, and to take all one's pluck out. I wonder the ladies are alive.'

'I can quite understand that,' Lord Halliburn said. 'I had no idea what it would be like until we got into it, and then, though the porters had brought up warm wraps for us, it was terrible. I should quite have given up hope had not the guides persisted that if you had got off the glacier you might have taken shelter somewhere under the lee of a rock, and that if so we might find you unharmed.'

'It was too late when we got off the glacier to think of it. The ladies were already almost insensible, and the rest of us so chilled to the bone that no shelter would have been of any use unless we could make a fire. That, of course, was out of the question, so our only chance was to make straight down the mountain. That was nothing to the work on the ice.'

'Hawtrey and Fortescue seem badly knocked up,' Lord Ulleswater said.

'Yes, they were completely exhausted by the time they got into that ravine. I don't think they could have gone much farther; they dropped off to sleep the instant we lighted the fire, and if we could not have done so I fancy they would never have woke again. The women bore up bravely as long as they had strength to struggle on. They literally went on until they dropped.'

'There is a mule here for you, Armstrong; indeed there are mules for all of us, for we brought six.'

'I am very glad to hear it, for I feel wonderfully shaky about the knees now it is all over.'

'No wonder,' Lord Ulleswater said; 'it is bad enough coming down the hill by oneself, but carrying a lady, it must have been hard work indeed.'

'I did not feel that much. The weight, well up on the shoulders, was nothing, and I kept so close behind the guide that I walked in his footsteps. I went on blindly, without thinking much about the path one way or the other; the thing that worried me most was that either Hawtrey or Fortescue might give out, and I could not think what we should do then. They stumbled very often, and I kept expecting to hear a fall. By the pace the guides went at I felt sure that we could carry the women down, and I thought that the warmth of our bodies would keep life in them; but if Hawtrey or Fortescue fell, I did not see what we should do. We could not leave him there to die, and yet to stop would have been death to all of us. Well, here are the mules, and I am not sorry for it.'

It was not until they were on something like level ground that they could quicken the pace of the animals. They were not long before they overtook the porters with the litters, and then, as they could do nothing there, they rode on ahead to see that everything was in readiness for their reception. With the exception of Captain Armstrong none of the party were able to leave their beds next day, but on the following morning Mr. Hawtrey and Mr. Fortescue were both up in time to say good-bye to Lord Halliburn and his friends, who were starting for Martigny. With the girls it was a longer matter. Clara Fortescue was delirious on the morning after their return, and an English doctor staying in the hotel at once pronounced it to be an attack of rheumatic fever; the other two had symptoms of the same malady, but these passed off, and on the fourth day both were able to get up, and on the following day were on sofas in the sitting-room.

'Well, you have made a nice business of it, young ladies,' Mr. Singleton said, when he paid them his first visit; 'this is what comes of mountaineering. You would have done much better to have stopped down here in the valley, instead of pretty nearly frightening us all to death, besides risking your own lives and injuring your health. I am glad to hear that your sister is a little better this morning, Miss Fortescue; the doctor thinks that the worst has passed, though she will still have a troublesome time of it.'

'I am sorry we frightened you all, Mr. Singleton,' Dorothy said.

'Well, Mrs. Fortescue and I had a bad time of it, Dorothy. Of course, we could not quite realise the danger, for down here the sun was shining brightly all the morning. I don't think Mrs. Fortescue did quite realise it until you arrived, but I knew the guides here would not have been so alarmed unless there had been real danger. I should have come up with the party but I knew that so far from being of the slightest use I should only have been a trouble to them. It was fortunate Halliburn and his two friends happened to be in the hotel; almost everyone else was out, and they took the management of the expedition in their hands, and hurried things up wonderfully. I never liked the man so much before as I did then. It was a tremendous relief when they rode in with Armstrong and brought us the news that you would be here in half an hour, and that although you were exhausted and worn out with the terrible time you had had they hoped that you would be none the worse for it. I think I realised what you had gone through most when your fathers came in, a quarter of an hour after you had been carried up to your rooms. They had to be lifted off their mules, and helped upstairs, where hot baths had been got ready for them, and if two strong, hearty men were so utterly exhausted, one could easily understand what a time you must have gone through.'

'Yes, but we were carried, Mr. Singleton,' Ada Fortescue said; 'I don't remember much about it, I was so cold and miserable, but I know that once I almost laughed at the thought that I was being carried like a package, on a guide's back, and what my mother would think of it if she saw me.'

'What did you feel, Dorothy?'

'I don't quite know what I felt,' she said reluctantly, and with somewhat heightened colour. 'I know I felt ashamed of myself; I used to think that I was as strong in my way as men are in theirs, and it seemed to me disgraceful that I should have to be carried. Then I could not help thinking, where the road was very steep, and I could hear the guide in front telling Captain Armstrong where he should step, that he might slip, and we should be both killed together. Otherwise, I felt safe, for I could tell that he was walking firmly, and was not feeling my weight too much. I don't think I lost consciousness at all; my body felt quite warm, but my hands and my feet were as if they were dead. I should not have been at all surprised to find that I had lost them altogether.'

In the afternoon Captain Armstrong was admitted to see the invalids. He at once laughed down Dorothy's attempt to thank him for having saved her life.

'I only did for you, Miss Hawtrey, exactly what the guides did for Miss Fortescue and her sister; there is nothing very terrible in carrying a weight when you get it comfortably fixed. Why, the porters in the Andes think nothing of carrying people right over the mountains; it is only a matter of getting weight properly balanced. I saw how the guides did; they knotted the shawls over their caps just above the peak. They carry weights here you know, as they do in most mountain countries, with a strap across the forehead. Coming over the ice I really did feel you heavy, though I had two others to help me with you, but the cold seemed to have taken all one's strength out of one, and the weight was all on one side; coming down was nothing in comparison. I believe I could have carried you right down to the hotel here with an occasional rest. I was as warm as a toast when we got into the wood. You must not think or say anything more about it; if you do I shall straightway pack up my kit and take my place in the next diligence wherever it may be going to. And now, were you able to walk into this room pretty easily?'

'We are both very stiff; I felt curiously weak, just as if I had had a long illness, but the doctor says it will soon pass off and that in a week we shall both be walking about again.'

'I rather think this will change our plans, Armstrong,' Mr. Hawtrey said; 'by the time we get back it will be far on in October and wetting damp and cold up in Lincolnshire, and the doctor advises me that it would be better to cross the Alps and spend a few weeks in Northern Italy, so as to set Dorothy completely up and to work the cold out of her system. I have not settled upon it yet, but I think that is probably what we will do. It is of no use running the risk of her getting rheumatism. But at any rate, we shall be here for another week or ten days, by which time I hope Clara Fortescue will have fairly turned the corner.' And so they lingered on.

In a week the two girls were able to get about again, to enjoy the sunshine in the valley. The hotel was nearly empty now, the season being over. Clara Fortescue was fairly through the fever, though still very weak; it was, however, only a question of time. Captain Armstrong still remained. Dorothy could no longer disguise from herself why he was staying. Up to the day of the expedition up to the Mer de Glace she had refused to admit the idea into her mind. She had before told him distinctly that she could never care for him in the way he wanted, and she had believed he had accepted the decision as final. They were great friends, and he had enjoyed their stay at Martigny just as she had done, and she had observed no difference in his manner to her or her two friends—in fact, if anything, she had thought, and was rather pleased than otherwise, that he was oftener by the side of Ada Fortescue than by her own.

There had been, however, something in his manner during that terrible time that had opened her eyes; something perhaps in the tone of his voice when he cheered her on, or in the clasp of his arm as he aided her father to carry her, that had told her the truth, and when he still lingered on at Chamounix she knew what was coming. What she did not know was what her answer would be. She liked him very much; he had saved her life; she was sure he would do his best to make her happy; and yet she did not feel that she loved him as she thought a woman should love a man who was to be her husband. She had made one mistake and had regretted it bitterly. She had become engaged without feeling that love, and had vowed to herself that never again would she say 'Yes' unless her whole heart went with her words. She had had her girlish hero, and for years had thought that no one was like him. Had he come back a little earlier, and had he still remained her ideal, she would never have become engaged to Lord Halliburn.

She had fancied that he was unchanged until a moment when he had failed in the perfect trust she had thought he had placed in her. Now he had gone away for months to America and that dream was over altogether. She had felt his journey as a personal grievance. Of course, after the offence he had given, it made no difference to her; she did not wish to see him; it was unpleasant for both of them. Nevertheless, she was somewhat sore at his acquiescing so readily in her decision that their old relations were entirely a thing of the past. In fact, she was unreasonable, and was vexed with herself for being so. It was annoying to her now that she should think of him at all. He had gone altogether out of her life, and would in a few months be back in India again; but the thought of the breach and its cause brought back again strongly to her the events of the two months previous to her leaving England.

These had been almost forgotten of late, but she acknowledged, as she thought it over, that her position was practically the same as it had been. She was still exposed to the charge of theft, and although it had been arranged that there should be a compromise, yet in the minds of the two tradesmen who had been victimised and of their assistants she was a thief, and although those who knew her best were convinced of her innocence, a whisper of the affair might yet get abroad, and were the facts known she would be generally condemned. Besides, at any moment the system might be recommenced, she might again be branded as a thief, and the tale of the compromise effected in the first cases would add weight to the charge. It was for this reason that she had broken off her engagement with Lord Halliburn, and had then declared to herself that never would she place herself in a similar position until she was absolutely and entirely cleared from all suspicion, and freed from any chance of a repetition of it.

Nothing had occurred to shake that determination. She had no right to enter upon any engagement until she stood above all suspicion. The man himself might trust her blindly, might scoff at the idea of her doing a dishonourable action, but that would not suffice to shield either him or her from the consequences of the charge. What a life would theirs be were she generally believed to be a thief. Society would close its doors against them. A consciousness of her innocence might support them, but the life would be none the less painful and humiliating. Dorothy arrived at this conclusion not without a certain amount of unacknowledged sense of relief. It obviated the necessity for giving a direct answer to the question that was to be asked her. She felt that she could not again say 'No,' yet she shrank from saying 'Yes'; so when, the next day, Captain Armstrong, happening to find her alone, told her that his love was unchanged since he had spoken to her in the spring, except that he loved her more, and asked if she could not give him a different answer to that with which she had sent him away, she said:

'I am sorry—so sorry, Captain Armstrong. It was a great pain to me to say "No" before, and if I had dreamt when you joined us at Martigny that you still thought of me in that way, I should have told you frankly at once that it were better for us both that you should not stay there; but I thought you had come to regard me as a friend, and it was not until that day on the ice I felt it was not so. It was a great pain to me to say "No" before. I liked you very much then, but, as I told you, not enough for that. I like you even more now; it would be impossible that I could help it when we have been so much together, and you did so much for me that day. I like you so much that if I were free ——' he would have broken in but she checked him by a motion of her hand.

'I am not otherwise than free in that way,' she said; 'I have broken off with Lord Halliburn for good and all, and yet I am not free. Had I been so I do not know what my answer would have been. I don't think I could have brought myself to say "No"; I feel sure I could hardly have said "Yes." I think I must have said, "I do not quite know." I have made one mistake; I must not make another. I like you very much, but I do not think that it is the love that a woman should give to her husband. Give me a little more time to think before I answer you.'

'I should have been well content, Dorothy; I would have waited as long as you liked; but I don't understand how it is that you are not free.'

'You have a right to know. It is because I am disgraced; because as long as this disgrace hangs over me I can never marry.'

'You mean those ridiculous stories that were in the papers, Dorothy. Do you think that I should care for a moment for such things as those, or that they have brought the slightest taint of disgrace upon you in the minds of those that know you?'

'That was the beginning of it,' she said, 'but there was worse; and it was that made me break off my engagement. I doubt now whether in any case I could have held to it. I had begun to feel I had made a mistake before that came, but even had I not done so it would have been the same. I am accused of theft.'

'Of theft, Dorothy!' he repeated in incredulous scorn. 'You suspected of theft!'

'And on evidence so strong,' she went on quietly, 'that even my father for a moment suspected me, and my dear friend, Mr. Singleton, believed that I had been mixed up in some disgraceful transaction; and others, who I thought knew me well, and would have trusted me, as I know you would have done, believed me guilty—not of theft, but of the previous accusations. There are shopmen in London ready to swear in a court of law that I obtained diamonds and other goods from them, and to-morrow fresh charges may be made, and ere long I may stand in the dock as a thief.'

Captain Armstrong looked at her as if he doubted her sanity.

'But no one in his senses could think such a thing, Dorothy.'

'But I have told you that even those who knew me best did, for a moment, think so. Mr. Charles Levine, the lawyer, is a clear-headed man, and yet even he, after hearing all the facts, was convinced of my guilt. I will tell you more —it is fair that I should do so,' and she gave him the history of the postcards, then of the robbery at the jeweller's, of Mr. Singleton lending her the money, of the other robbery on the same day, and of Captain Hampton seeing her in conversation on that afternoon with the man they believed to be the author of the postcards.

'You see,' she said, 'that here is the evidence of three or four tradespeople, all of whom know me well by sight, and who recognised my dress as well as my face. Here is the evidence of Mr. Singleton, who has known me from a child, and that of Captain Hampton, who was at the time seeing me every day; and to all this I have but to oppose my own denial, and to declare that I never was at any of the four places that afternoon.'

'I should believe your word if a thousand swore to the contrary,' he said passionately.

'You may now when you have heard all these things,' she said, 'but you would not at the time. When the shopkeeper and his assistant told my father that story I could see that his face turned white, and that for a moment he believed that I must have taken these things in order to obtain money to bribe the man whom I had solemnly declared had no letters of mine. When I heard the story told, and that my very dress was recognised, I asked myself if I could have done it unconsciously, in a state of somnambulism or something of that sort. I was absolutely dazed and bewildered. With all your trust in me I am sure you must have been shaken when you heard that story, just as my own father was. Again, when my old and kindest friend, Mr. Singleton, declared that I had come to him sobbing and crying, and begging him to save me from disgrace, and that he had given me a cheque for a thousand pounds, could he be blamed for believing that the girl he knew and loved had been engaged in some scandalous affair? As to Captain Hampton, he believed me absolutely in regard to the letters, but he doubted me afterwards. Try to put yourself in his place. If you had known about this affair of the letters, and you had seen me in an out-of-the-way part of London, engaged in a conversation with the man we were searching for as the author of the postcards, what would you have thought?' She asked the question a little wistfully.

'I can't say,' he said honestly. 'I suppose just for a moment I must have thought you had really got into some serious sort of scrape. I don't see how I could have helped it. I am sure I should never have thought you had done anything really wrong.'

'But in that case I should have been a liar.'

'I don't suppose I should have thought of that at the time, Dorothy. When I came to think it all over I should have said it was impossible, and should have doubted my own senses; but the robbery I never could have believed in, if a hundred shopkeepers had sworn to it. But what does it all really mean? There must be some explanation of it all.'

'The only explanation we can arrive at,' she replied, 'is that there is some other woman so like me that she can pass for me when dressed up in clothes like my own.'

'Of course, of course. What a fool I was not to think of that.'

'Yes, Captain Armstrong, you accept it, just as my father and Mr. Singleton accept it, because you and they would accept anything rather than believe me guilty; but would anyone else believe it if I went into court, and this mass of evidence was brought against me? What would my bare denial weigh against it? Would the suggestion of my counsel that the theft had been committed by some other woman, so like me that even those who knew me best had been deceived, unsupported as it would be by even a shadow of evidence, be accepted for an instant? You know well enough that the jury would return a verdict against me without a moment's hesitation, and that all the world, save some half-a-dozen people, would believe me guilty.

'At present, the police all over England are endeavouring to find proofs of the existence of my double. A notice has been sent to every country in Europe. This has been going on ever since we left England, and, so far, without the slightest success. After having been so successful it is hardly likely that the thing will not be attempted again, and in that case it must come before the public. It will be terrible to bear the disgrace alone, but it would be ten times more so did it involve another in my disgrace. Do not pain me by saying more, Captain Armstrong,' and she laid her hand on his arm as he was about to speak, 'nothing could induce me to change my determination. If at any time this dreadful mystery is cleared up, should you come to me again, I will give you an honest answer. I do not say it will be "Yes." It must be as my heart will decide then. At present my hope is that you will not wait for that: the matter may never be cleared up. I believe, myself, that it never will be, and I would far rather know that you were married to some woman who would make you as happy as you deserve, than that you were wasting your life on me, and that even should I be cleared I might not be able to give you the answer you want.'

'I will wait for a time, at any rate, Dorothy,' he said quietly; 'but I will not say more now. You are very good to have spoken so frankly to me. I ought not to have allowed you to talk so much. I can see that it has been almost too great a strain for you. I think that I had better leave to-morrow morning.'

'I think it will be best,' she said; 'but promise me, Captain Armstrong, that in any case we shall always be good friends. You may think little of the act of saving my life, but I shall never forget it. You promised me before that I should find no change in your manner, and you kept your word well.'

'I promise you again, Dorothy,' he said, raising her hand to his lips, 'if I am never to regard you in a closer light, I shall always think of you as my dearest friend.'

'And I shall rejoice in your happiness as a sister might do, Captain Armstrong;' and in a minute he was gone, and Dorothy, sitting down, indulged in a long cry. She did not attempt to analyse her feelings; she was not sure whether she was glad or sorry, whether she had virtually refused him or not; she was certainly relieved that she had not been obliged to make up her mind to give an answer from which there would have been no drawing back. Half an hour later her father came in.

'The carriage will be at the door in ten minutes, my dear. You are looking pale, child; are you not feeling so well?'

'I have rather a headache. I think instead of going for a drive I will lie down until dinner-time.'

She came down looking herself again. She knew that Captain Armstrong's intention of leaving the next morning would excite a certain amount of surprise, and that it possibly might be suspected that she was not unconnected with his departure. Certainly Ada Fortescue would have her suspicions, for during the last two or three days she had thrown out some little hints that showed that she was not blind as to his intentions. She was relieved to find as she sat down that the party were in ignorance of his approaching departure. It was not until the meal was nearly finished that Captain Armstrong said suddenly:

'I have been putting off tearing myself away from day to day, but my leave is up, and I am afraid I cannot possibly delay any longer. It goes awfully against the grain, but there is no help for it, and I have been to the office this afternoon and booked my place for Geneva to-morrow morning.'

There was a general chorus of regret.

'I mustn't grumble,' he said laughingly. 'I have had a very pleasant time indeed, though I have not gone in as I had intended for mountaineering. I think my one mild attempt that way has a good deal quenched my ardour. I ought to have gone ten days ago, but I did not like to do so until Miss Fortescue was up and fairly on the way to recover her strength. I am glad to have had the pleasure of seeing her to-day. That has, however, knocked from under me my last excuse for remaining here any longer. I shall get a severe wigging as it is for exceeding my leave. Of course, I have written, making various excuses, but it won't do any longer, and I shall have to travel right through without a stay. I hope, Mrs. Fortescue, that I shall meet you all in London in a few weeks' time, and find your daughter quite herself again. I suppose, Mr. Hawtrey, I shall have to look forward to the beginning of the season before I see you and Miss Hawtrey?'

'I think it likely we shall not be in town until May,' Mr. Hawtrey replied. 'We shall probably work down so as to be at Rome at Easter, and shall have a month or two of quiet at home before we come up to town; still that must depend on circumstances. If you can get a few days' leave later on, I should be very pleased if you could run down to my place for a week's shooting. There has not been a gun fired there this season; take a couple of men down with you if you like. I will write to my housekeeper and the gamekeeper, saying that you are to be looked after just the same as if we were at home, and all you will have to do will be to send her a note, saying that you are coming, a couple of days beforehand. Her name is Brodrick—make a note of that in your pocket-book.'

'Thank you, I shall enjoy it very much if I can get away. I have my doubts whether I shall be able to; but if I can, I will certainly avail myself of your offer.'

'So it was "no," Dorothy,' Ada Fortescue whispered as they went upstairs together that night. 'I knew that by his face this afternoon; he tried to talk and laugh as usual, but I could see things had gone badly with him. You need not tell me if you don't like,' she went on, as Dorothy gave no answer. 'It is not a difficult riddle to guess for oneself.'

'I will tell you, but it must be quite to yourself, Ada; there were certain reasons why I could give him no answer at all. No, you don't understand it,' she went on, in answer to Ada's look of surprise. 'I don't suppose you ever will, but there are circumstances that render it impossible for me to give him an answer, and as far as I can see there is not likely to be any alteration in those circumstances; so please do not say anything more about it. He himself sees that I could not act differently, and I think most likely that the question will never be asked again. Perhaps some day or other I may tell you about it. We have got to be real friends now, and when you do hear you will acknowledge that I have done right. Good-night now; I am so glad to think that Clara is to be down to breakfast again in the morning.'

This was not the only conversation on the subject. Mr. Singleton, contrary to his usual custom, sat up until all but Mr. Hawtrey bad retired.

'That has been a bit of a surprise, Hawtrey. There is no doubt that he has proposed, and that she has not accepted him, as I had quite made up my mind she would do.'

'Do you think so? The idea had not occurred to me. They both seemed just the same as usual.'

'You are as blind as a bat, Hawtrey. Didn't she stay at home with a headache this afternoon? and isn't he going away suddenly to-morrow? It does not require the smallest degree of penetration to discover what that means. It is a relief to me—a great relief; but I am afraid it is only a postponement. She has refused to accept him on the same grounds that she broke off her engagement to the other man. Now I think it over I see it is about the only thing she could have done. It would not have been right to have become engaged as long as this thing is hanging over her. It is all very well for you and I to feel that we are going to compromise the matter comfortably; but there it is still, and may break out afresh again at any moment. She has shaken it off a bit since we came away, but it must be on her mind, and I expect she frankly told

Armstrong why she could give him no answer at present. Still, I am afraid it will come to the same thing in the long run.'

Mr. Hawtrey wisely held his tongue. He himself would have been in every way content with Captain Armstrong as a son-in-law, but as he had no wish to irritate his friend, he abstained from going farther into the subject.

CHAPTER XVIII

Mr. Singleton had gone out for a stroll after breakfast with Dorothy and Ada Fortescue. Mrs. Fortescue was with Clara, who had come down to breakfast for the first time and was now lying down for a bit as a preparation for going for a short drive later on. Mr. Hawtrey was smoking a cigar in front of the hotel with Mr. Fortescue, intending to follow the girls and Mr. Singleton after the post came in. After half an hour's waiting the bag for the hotel was brought in.

'They are principally yours, Fortescue,' Mr. Hawtrey said, as the clerk sorted them over. 'The inquiries after Clara's health must have materially benefited the postal revenue. As you are not coming I will put those four for Ada in my pocket. There is nothing for either of the others, and only one for me. I know what its contents are without opening it.'

Putting the five letters into his pocket, he strolled down the village. He knew exactly where he should find the others, as they almost always took their seat in a nook sheltered completely from the wind and exposed to the full rays of the sun.

'I suppose I had better look at the letter,' he said to himself. 'I would rather Danvers did not write so often. Dorothy looks up inquiringly whenever the post comes in, and I would rather say "No letter to-day," than to have to say, "There is a letter from Danvers, Dorothy, but he sends no news whatever." It comes to the same thing, no doubt, but no letter might mean that they had got some little clue and meant following it up. At any rate, she does not look so disappointed as when I tell her that there is a letter with nothing in it.'

'Hulloa!' he exclaimed, as he opened it, 'this is a much more lengthy epistle.' The first line or two were sufficient to cause him to burst into something like a shout of joy. They ran:—'I am delighted to be able to give you the good news that the existence and whereabouts of the man and the counterfeit of Miss Hawtrey have been ascertained without a doubt. Hampton was right when he considered they would probably have made off to the United States directly they had secured their plunder. I received a letter from him this morning. Unfortunately I have been away shooting for a week, and it has been lying unopened since the day I left.' Then followed a copy of Captain Hampton's letter, together with copies of the various affidavits.

'These prove practically all we require. I have been round with them to Charles Levine. He is very much gratified, and says that he considers this testimony should be ample to enable us to defend any action on the part of

Gilliat. He thinks the best plan will be to place Captain Hampton's letter and the depositions before Gilliat and say that we are prepared to defend the action and to bring over all these people as witnesses. Of course, it would be more satisfactory to have the adventuress and her accomplice in the dock or to produce their written confession. Such is evidently Hampton's opinion also. You see he has started for New Orleans and says he shall follow them if he has to cross the continent. This, however, I have not copied, as he has put that on a separate piece of paper and marked it private and confidential. From something he said to me the day before he started I imagine he has for some reason or other an objection to Miss Hawtrey's knowing that he is working on her behalf.

'You see, in the early part of the letter, which he thought would be sent to you, and doubtless shown to her, he treats the discovery he has made as a purely accidental matter, although he told me that he intended to make it his sole business to hunt them down, if it took him six months to do so. However, when he wrote he was certainly on the point of starting for New Orleans, and I own that I consider his undertaking to be a somewhat perilous one. This fellow must be a thorough-paced ruffian, and he will find no difficulty in getting together any number of reckless men who would, if they found he was in danger of arrest, hesitate at nothing. Of course, if he goes farther west his errand will be still more difficult. Hampton is so thoroughly good a fellow that I should feel grieved indeed did anything befall him.'

Mr. Hawtrey thrust the letter and enclosure into his pocket and hurried on; he hesitated for a moment, as he remembered that Ada Fortescue was with his daughter, but he said to himself, 'She is a good girl and a great friend of Dorothy's; we can trust her to hold her tongue—besides, we need not go much into the past.'

'Why, you've been running, father?'

'No, my dear, no; but I am a little excited over a letter I have just received. It is a family matter, Ada, but I know Dorothy will not wish you to go away, for I am sure we can trust you with our little secret.'

'Have you news, father?' Dorothy asked, springing to her feet. 'News about that?'

'Yes, dear; but first I must tell your friend that some tradesmen have been robbed by a person so strongly resembling you that she deceived even those that knew you well. The matter was so serious that we have had a number of detectives searching for this woman, as only by her being found could we prove that the orders for these goods were not given by you. Having told her that much I can go on with my news.

'They have been found, Dorothy. Thank God they have been found!'

The girl threw her arms round her father's neck and burst into a passion of tears. Hitherto she had had nothing but her consciousness of innocence to support her. Until the suggestion had been made by Captain Hampton that some one had impersonated her, she had been in a state of complete bewilderment, and even this hypothesis seemed to her to be improbable in the extreme. Still as her father and Mr. Singleton had accepted it, she, too, had clung to it, but with less real hope than they had entertained, that it might prove to be true.

As the weeks had passed by without any shadow of proof that such a person existed being forthcoming, she had more than once told herself that she would have to pass all her life with this dark cloud over her. A few close friends might believe in her, but when the story was whispered about, as sooner or later it would be sure to be, everyone else would hold aloof from her. She had been feeling that morning in lower spirits than usual. Captain Armstrong had left early, and she was deeply sorry for him, more sorry for him than for herself. She had slept but little that night, and had come to the conclusion that were this weight ever removed and were he ever to ask her again, her life would be a happy one with him, even though she did not feel for him more than a very real liking. The sudden announcement of a fact she herself had begun to doubt, for a time completely upset her, and her father at last said, 'I will leave you here for a few minutes with your friend, Dorothy, and will stroll away with Singleton. By the time we return you will be able to listen calmly to the story.'

When they had gone a short distance away from the girls, he placed the copies of the letters and depositions in Mr. Singleton's hands.

'Hampton!' the latter exclaimed, as soon as he glanced over the first line or two; 'I am glad indeed. Let us sit down on that rock over there; the news is too pleasant to be lost by not being able to read it distinctly.'

'Well, Hawtrey, I congratulate you,' he said, when he had finished. 'Those letters are sufficient to prove to any unprejudiced person that Dorothy has been perfectly innocent throughout the whole business. It is a pity the birds had flown before Hampton arrived there. Even putting everything else aside, I would have given something to see that woman who humbugged me so completely. What will our young lady say now when she hears that it is Hampton who has thus cleared her? By the way, he writes as if it were a mere accident, his having discovered them.'

'I fancy he writes in that style because he has no doubt that she will see the letter. There is the letter Danvers sent me with the enclosure. Hampton seems to be just as obstinate about the matter as Dorothy is.'

Mr. Singleton read the letter with many grunts of disapprobation.

'Why couldn't he be satisfied with what he has done?' he exclaimed, when he had finished the letter. 'He had got enough evidence to satisfy any reasonable people; now he must needs go chasing them all over America, and as likely as not get shot for his pains. Why didn't he write over and ask whether that was not sufficient?'

'Because if he had done so, Singleton, he might never have been able to pick up the clue again. The evidence he has got may not be absolutely conclusive, but undoubtedly it will be very valuable. These affidavits prove conclusively that there was on a certain day a woman staying in a New York Hotel who was so like Dorothy that my daughter's portrait was believed by several people who had seen the woman to be hers. It could also be proved that she and the man with her had just come from Hamburg. But you see it does not in any way connect this woman with the robbery. There is the weak point of the business. The evidence is enough, as you say, to convince reasonable people; but as these shopmen are all ready to swear to Dorothy, the fact that we have found a woman exactly like her, but whom we cannot produce, is scarcely a satisfactory proof from a legal point of view that she is innocent. However, we can talk that over presently; we had better join the others; Dorothy will be wanting to hear the news. Be careful what you say; we may both think that Ned Hampton's views are foolish, but we are bound to respect them.'

Mr. Singleton made no reply, and mentally resolved that if it were necessary he would speak about it, whether or no.

'I am not going to see the young fool throw away his chances like that,' he said to himself; 'he does not know what has been going on here—that Dorothy has been within an ace of accepting some one else. All this foolery of his shows that he really cares for her. If he had not done so he would simply have laughed at her nonsense.'

They met the girls coming towards them.

'You have been an unconscionable time, father, I am burning with impatience to know how it has all come about.'

'Those papers will tell you, Dorothy. One is an extract from a letter written to Mr. Danvers by Ned Hampton, the others are copies of affidavits sworn in New York.'

Dorothy changed colour. She had been thinking of her former friend that night, and had very reluctantly come to the conclusion that she had been unduly hard upon him. She had asked Captain Armstrong what he would have thought had he seen her as Ned Hampton had supposed that he had done, and in spite of his love for her and his absolute confidence in her word, Captain Armstrong had admitted that he should at first have come to exactly the same conclusion—namely, that she had got into a scrape.

She had not felt either hurt or angry when he admitted this. Why, then, should she have been both in the case of her old playfellow? The question was altogether an unwelcome one, and she had dismissed it as speedily as possible, but the name coming upon her now so suddenly and unexpectedly had almost startled her. In some anger against herself for the involuntary flush, she took the papers and prepared to read them much more deliberately than she would otherwise have done.

However, her eyes ran over the lines more rapidly as she read on, and when she finished she exclaimed—

'What a wonderful piece of good fortune! It seems quite providential that Captain Hampton should have taken a fancy to go out to America, and should have inquired when he went through New York if this man and woman had lately arrived. He seems to have managed wonderfully well; it was lucky he got such a clever detective as the person he speaks of. Really, father, I feel very grateful to him.'

'So I think you ought to,' Mr. Hawtrey said somewhat sharply, 'considering that he has done what all the detectives in London have failed to do, even aided by the police all over the Continent, and has gone a long way towards lifting a cloud, which, if it had not been for him, would have darkened your whole life.'

'I quite feel that, father; I have been thinking that over while you have been away, and have told Ada that no words can express what a relief it is to me. Of course, I am very, very grateful to Captain Hampton; it was very good of him, indeed, to think of me, and to take such trouble about me. What shall we have to do next?'

'That must depend upon what the lawyers say, Dorothy; I almost wish that we had been going back to London, so as to talk it over with them personally.'

'Why shouldn't we go, father? I am feeling quite well again now, and am wanting very much to be home again. I would infinitely rather do that than go to Italy. The Fortescues are talking of starting in a couple of days, why should we not all go back together?'

'I will think it over, my dear. Now, I think you had better be getting back to the hotel; the sun has gone in and the clouds are half-way down the mountains. I think that we are going to have another snowstorm, so you and

Ada had better hurry. You have had experience of the suddenness with which storms come on here.'

'I suppose this was why you would give no answer yesterday?' Ada Fortescue said, as the two girls walked briskly back toward Chamounix, followed more leisurely by Mr. Hawtrey and his friend.

'Yes, partly, Ada.'

'What a pity the news did not come a day sooner.'

'I don't know, Ada, I really had not made up my mind. You see, all along I have been feeling that I could never get engaged again, and so I had an answer ready, and had not thought it over as I should have done otherwise. There is a snowflake. Do let us hurry, so as to be in before it begins in earnest.'

Ada did not see the snowflake, but she saw that her companion wanted to change the subject, and nothing more was said till they reached the hotel, just as the snow was really beginning to fall.

Dorothy remained for some time in her room. She was dissatisfied with herself for not feeling more elated at the discovery that had been made. It was everything to her, she told herself; the greatest event of her life; and yet, after the first burst of joy, it had not made her as happy as it should have done.

It was tiresome that it should have been made by Captain Hampton. She had requested him not to interfere farther in her affairs. He had done so, and with success.

Certainly she would much rather that this woman had been discovered by some one else. But this was not all. If the news had come a day earlier she supposed that she should have accepted Captain Armstrong, and there would have been an end of it. She had promised that she would let him know if this was ever cleared up. Now, in honour she ought to write to him. Anyhow, there was no occasion for that to-day. He had only left that morning; it would look ridiculous were he to get her letter the day he arrived in town. If they were going back she could wait until they were in England. It would be a difficult letter to write, most difficult; and she sat down for a time thinking, and ended by being as unjustly angry with Captain Armstrong as she had been with Ned Hampton.

'I believe I am getting quite idiotic,' she said, getting up impatiently. 'I shall begin to think that storm on the glacier has affected my brain. When I ought to be the happiest girl possible, here I am discontented with everything.'

The result of the conversation between Mr. Hawtrey and his friend was that at luncheon the former announced that a letter that he had received that morning told him his presence was required in London, and as Dorothy was so much better, he should give up the idea of a visit to Italy, and should go home with her at once.

'Let us all go together,' Clara said. 'I am sure that I am strong enough to travel, and I do so long to be home.'

As it was agreed that a couple of days could make no difference to her, orders were at once given for the carriages to be ready the next morning, and at an early hour they started on their way down to Geneva.

CHAPTER XIX

Mr. Hawtrey made but a few hours' stay in London, Dorothy urging her father to leave at once for home. He would have preferred stopping for a day or two to confer with Mr. Charles Levine, and to get the matter with the jeweller settled before he went North, but Dorothy pressed the point so much that he gave way.

'What is the use, father,' she urged, 'of employing people to do your law business and then doing it yourself? I should think when Gilliat sees a copy of those papers Mr. Danvers sent us, he will be convinced that he has been wrong all through, but even if he isn't, you could not argue the matter with him. Mr. Levine could say a great deal more than you could. I quite understand, from what you told me, that there is really nothing to connect this woman with the theft; still, anyone could see that it would be more likely that she should do it than I should.'

'Except this, Dorothy—that you were in London at the time, and there is no proof that she was; and that these people all swear it was you, while the most that we can prove is that there is in existence some one who is wonderfully like you. It is an immense satisfaction to us to have got as far as we have. We have, at any rate, a strong defence, and the story will at least satisfy all who know you. Still, Singleton agrees with me that a jury would hardly be satisfied, and that the verdict would probably be against us.

'I don't expect the jeweller to give up his claim. I don't think it would be reasonable to expect it. The man has been robbed of valuable goods, and he and his two assistants were absolutely convinced that it was you who took them. There were reports about that you were being pressed for money; and our defence that a woman, so like you that your portrait was taken for hers, crossed from Hamburg to New York a week after the robbery, cannot be taken as conclusive that it was this woman and not you who was at the jeweller's shop. My greatest comfort in the matter is at present that this woman is at the other side of the Atlantic, and I am quite prepared to meet the jeweller half-way and share the loss with him if Levine does not think that in case this woman does return, as it is almost certain she will do, and attempts similar frauds, my having compromised the matter would weaken our position.'

'I see all that, father, but I don't see why you should not write about it to Mr. Levine, instead of going into it with him personally. He is sure to want you to stay in town, and then there is no saying how long we might be kept. You will be up in town again in the spring.'

'Very well, Dorothy, we will start to-morrow morning. If Levine thinks it is absolutely necessary he should see me I must run up again. The train takes us so far towards home now that it is only eighteen hours' travelling, and I must own that I shall be heartily glad to be at home again. We have been away more than eight months, which is longer than I can remember having been from home all my life.'

Mr. Singleton was glad when his friend told him that they would travel down together.

'I would rather have stayed a couple of days, Singleton, but Dorothy has set her mind upon starting at once.'

'I don't wonder at that; she has had a rough time of it altogether, and must long for the quiet of home; besides, as you know, my theory is that she refused to give any decided answer to Armstrong because of this business. I should not be at all surprised if she is afraid he might get to know she is in town and might call to see her, and she wants to have time to think it over quietly before she has to give him a decided answer one way or the other.'

'But you thought she would accept him, Singleton; you told me you had quite made up your mind that she would do so.'

'Yes, I am almost sure that if it had not been for the affair of the diamonds she would have done so any time during that last fortnight at Chamounix; but, you see, she was under the spell of the place then, and of the adventure on the glacier. She considered he had saved her life, and no doubt he did, though I do not say the guides might not have managed it somehow if left to themselves; still, we may put it that he saved her. Of course that went for a great deal with her; before that I don't think she thought about it. I watched her closely, and there was really no difference in her manner to him and to Fitzwarren. She looked upon them both simply as pleasant companions. I saw the change directly afterwards. Then there is no denying he is a very good fellow in all respects, and likely to take with ninety-nine girls out of a hundred, so that I have no doubt she would have accepted him if it had not been for this other business. Now, of course, she has been away from him a week. The jewel business has to a great extent been cleared up. At any rate, there is an explanation consistent with her innocence, which there was not before, and she is therefore face to face with the question—shall she accept Armstrong? She wants to think it over, and does not want to be pressed; therefore, she is in a fever to get away down into the country, before he can know that she has come back. I believe it will come to the same thing. Perhaps she told him she would take him if she felt free to do so. At any rate, Hampton has put himself out of the running by his own folly, and I have nothing more to say on the matter. However, I am glad we are all going back together.'

Accordingly the next morning they started by train, slept at Nottingham that night, and then posted the remaining sixty miles.

Mr. Hawtrey saw with satisfaction that as soon as Dorothy took up her own life again, her spirits, which had been very uneven since she left Switzerland, began to return. There was much to occupy her—all her pensioners in the village to visit, hours to be spent with the head gardener in the greenhouses and conservatories, walks to be taken with the dogs, and the horses to be visited and petted. Into all this she threw herself with her whole energy. Her father had written a long letter to Danvers on the morning after his return; ten days later the reply came.

> 'My dear sir,—I have bad news to give you. I have been away on the Continent for a fortnight, and only received your letter this morning, and at the same time, one from Hampton. It was a long chatty letter, giving me an amusing account of his voyage to New Orleans. It was written a few hours after he landed there, and he said that he was writing because the mail went out next day, and he should keep it open in case he had any news to send me. It is finished by some one else. Where Ned left off are a few scrambling misspelt words, so badly written that I had the greatest difficulty in making them out. I transcribe them as sent.'

> 'Sir,—This hear is to tel you has the Captin as got a-stabed by a niggur last nite, he his very bad but the docters thinks he will git hover it. —JACOB.'

'What is it, father?' Dorothy asked, as he uttered an exclamation of regret.

'It is from Danvers, my dear. He writes to tell me that he hears that Ned Hampton has been badly hurt—stabbed, it seems, by some negro.'

Dorothy turned very pale, and set down the teapot hastily.

'He is not killed, father?'

'No; the person who writes says he is very bad, but the doctors think he will get over it. Nothing more is known about it, he says. Hampton wrote him a long, chatty letter, which he left unfinished, as the post was not going out until next day. It was finished by some one else—a few misspelt words'—and he read Jacob's addition.

'Here is a bit more. "As Hampton told me before he started that he had taken a boy with him, as a sort of servant, I have just been to his old lodgings in Jermyn Street, and find that the lad's name was Jacob. It is a satisfaction to know that Hampton has some one with him who is attached to him, even if only a boy, as I have no doubt this lad is, for Hampton almost picked him off the street. I will let you know as soon as I hear again."'

'This is a very bad business, Dorothy.'

'Very bad, father. I am indeed sorry. How could he have got into a quarrel with a negro?'

'That is more than I can tell, dear. I would give a great deal if this hadn't happened. I have an immense liking for the young fellow. I was fond of him as a boy and he has grown up just as I thought he would—a man one can rely upon in every emergency—clear-headed, sensible, without a shadow of nonsense about him, and as true as steel. There, I can eat no more breakfast,' and he pushed his plate from him and rising hastily left the room. Dorothy went about the house with a pale face all day. Her father rode off directly after breakfast to carry the news to Singleton who was greatly distressed thereat.

'Did you tell Dorothy that it was at New Orleans?' he asked presently.

'No, I did not mention the place. I thought it was as well to wait until we got another letter. Of course she knew from those affidavits that the man and woman had gone down there.'

'I would have told her,' Mr. Singleton said. 'Ned begged us to say nothing about it, and though I did not give any specific promise, I have held my tongue thus far, though I have been strongly inclined to tell her a dozen times; but there is no reason why she should not know it was New Orleans. If she likes to put two and two together, she can. I wonder whether this attack on him had anything to do with our affair.'

'That is what I was thinking as I rode over, Singleton. I don't see how it could have done so. You see he had only just arrived there—but there is no saying; the boy distinctly says it was a nigger, and it may only have been an attempt at robbery. I suppose the letter was written in the evening. If the boat had come in early he would have set about making inquiries at once, but as he was evidently leaving it until the next day, I take it he must have written after dinner and then gone out for a stroll and perhaps got stabbed by some vagabond or other for the sake of his watch.'

'How did Dorothy take it?'

'She seemed very sorry; but, in fact, I did not notice much. I was regularly upset, and got out of the room as soon as I could, for if I had talked about it I should have broken down. Poor lad, to think of his having gone through half-a-dozen desperate fights in India and then to be stabbed by a negro thief at New Orleans.'

'Evidently the boy thought there was some hope,' Mr. Singleton said; 'so we must trust that the next letter will bring better news. I cannot bring myself to believe that we are going to lose Ned Hampton in this way.'

The days passed quietly. Dorothy had put off writing to Captain Armstrong, telling herself that there was no hurry, for although, if he met the Fortescues, he might learn she had returned to England, he would not know that any change had occurred in reference to the matter of which she had spoken to him. She had asked her father on the evening on which the letter came to let her read it, and although she had said nothing on the subject had not failed to notice that it was at New Orleans he had been wounded. She knew enough of America to be aware that he could not have gone there on his way to the districts where he might be going to shoot game, and she wondered whether he had really gone down there in order to find out something more about this woman.

It was very good of him if he had done so, and had put aside his own plans for the purpose. She had lately been thinking of him with a good deal of contrition. He had really taken a great deal of pains to try and find this man, and that after she had been so angry with him he should have pursued his inquiries in New York, had given her a sharp pang, and had opened her eyes still more widely to the injustice with which she had treated him. He had only spent a day over it; but still, it had showed that her affairs still occupied his mind; but if he had really given up his plans in order to follow these people down to New Orleans, it was a real sacrifice, and one that she felt she had not deserved.

She did not admit to herself that this had anything whatever to do with the delay in writing to Captain Armstrong, any more than she had admitted that she had been prevented from writing at once from Chamounix by any thought of Ned. She did acknowledge to herself that if Ned Hampton was to die of this wound, which he never would have received had he not gone down to New Orleans on her business, it would be a matter of deep regret to her all her life. She shrank from speaking of him, and the subject was never alluded to, unless her father or Mr. Singleton spoke of it, which they always did when the latter came over, and she then seldom joined in the conversation.

It was nearly a month later when Mr. Hawtrey one morning found among his letters one from Danvers. Three or four letters had passed between them. Mr. Levine had seen the jeweller, who, although admitting that the evidence of the existence of another person who strongly resembled Miss Hawtrey was remarkable, pointed out the absence of any proof whatever that this person had even been in London at the time the diamonds were taken away, and declaring that his own impressions remained unchanged. At the same time, he was perfectly ready to let the matter remain open for a year or more if necessary, and would, indeed, much rather do so than accept any offer for part payment or even for entire payment from Mr. Hawtrey.

It seemed highly probable that proof would by that time be obtained that might clear the matter up entirely. If he had been the subject of an extraordinarily clever fraud he was willing to submit to the entire loss, and would, indeed, hail with satisfaction any evidence that would convince him that he and his assistants had been deceived, and would thus entirely clear away the unjust suspicion that he could not otherwise but feel of a young lady who was the daughter of an old and valued customer of the firm.

'The man speaks fairly enough, I must confess,' Danvers had written; 'he is evidently absolutely convinced that he and his assistants cannot have made a mistake as to the lady who visited them. He was, of course, much struck at the depositions from New York, but remarked that people are liable to be deceived by photographs, that it is one thing to see a likeness, perhaps accidental, between a photograph and a living person, but another altogether to mistake a living person you know well for another. He is evidently greatly disturbed and troubled over the affair. He said over and over again, "I would infinitely rather lose the money and that Miss Hawtrey should be cleared; but, upon the other hand, I cannot give way without evidence that will absolutely convince me that my senses have been deceived in so extraordinary a manner."'

Mr. Hawtrey, then, expected no news of any importance from Danvers as to his affairs, but it was possible the letter might contain some later intelligence from New Orleans. It was nearly a month since they had heard, and in a case like this no news is very far from being good news; he opened it, therefore, with great reluctance, the more so that the letter was lying at the top of the others, and he saw by the anxiety with which Dorothy was watching him that she had at once recognised the handwriting. As his eye fell upon the contents he uttered an exclamation of thankfulness.

'It is from Ned himself,' Mr. Hawtrey said. 'Thank God for that!'

Dorothy repeated the exclamation of thankfulness in a low tone; her hands moved unsteadily among the tea-things in front of her and then she suddenly burst into tears.

Her father went round to her. 'There, there, my child,' he said, putting his hand on her shoulder, 'do not distress yourself. I know that you must have been as anxious as I have for the last month, as to the fate of your old friend, though you have chosen to keep it to yourself. I know that you must have felt it even more from having treated him unjustly before he went away.'

'I shall be better directly, father; it is very silly.'

'It is not silly at all, Dorothy,' he said, as he went back to his seat; 'it is only natural that you should have been anxious when you knew a friend was lying dangerously wounded, and that you should be upset now that you hear of his recovery. I will glance through the letter and tell you what he says.'

Danvers had written but a few lines with the letter.

'My dear Mr. Hawtrey,—I enclose Hampton's letter, which speaks for itself. I think that his conjecture as to the author of the attempt on his life is likely to be correct, and much as I should be glad to hear that your daughter was finally and satisfactorily cleared from these charges, I cannot but regret that Hampton should have undertaken so dangerous a business as that upon which he has embarked. I think it better to send you his letter, especially as we are not likely to hear again from him for a long time.'

Ned Hampton's letter commenced with an expression of regret that his friend should have been unduly alarmed about him by his boy having sent off the letter with an addition of his own. 'Of course he meant well, but it was a pity he did it. The wound was a severe one and no doubt I had a very narrow escape of my life. I was rising from my seat as the fellow struck at me from behind. That movement saved my life, for the bowie knife—a formidable weapon in use here—went down to the handle between my shoulder-bone and my ribs. That is, I take it, the plain English of the surgeon's technical explanation. The boy did his best, and sprang at the negro as I fell, and got a blow on the top of his head with the handle of the knife. It stunned him and made a nasty scalp wound, and would probably have killed him if it had not glanced off. The scoundrel only got a few dollars, for I had fortunately emptied my pockets of valuables before leaving the hotel.'

The writer then went on to state that he had discovered that the people they were in search of 'had left their hotel suddenly half an hour after I had landed. They had taken a passage up the river, and there seemed no reason for their sudden departure. Putting that and the attack together I can't help thinking that there must be some connection between them. The attack alone might have been accounted for. It is a lawless sort of place, and seating myself as I did on the deserted wharf, any ruffian who noticed me might have considered me a likely victim, just as he might have in any city of Europe; but the fact of these people leaving so suddenly rather alters the case, and I cannot help thinking that Truscott must have been among the crowd on the wharf when the steamer went in, and that he recognised me.

'He may have noticed me with the Hawtreys at the Oaks, or I may have been pointed out to him that day I saw him and followed him; he may have been watching the house in Chester Square, and have seen me come out; he may have noticed me walking with Mr. Hawtrey. If he did recognise me it would account for his sudden departure; and as I find that he had an intimate acquaintance in New Orleans, he may have left him to take steps to effectually prevent further pursuit. They are bound, as I found out by the outfit they bought here, for California; they go up the Missouri to Omaha, and start from there in a waggon across the plains. What they intend to do there I cannot, of course, say; the only clue I have is that the police have discovered for me that the man they went about with, whose name was Murdoch, was the keeper of a low saloon here, frequented by sailors and a low class of gamblers. He sold his place three or four days before he started, and has gone up with them. His name is on the list of passengers, so it may be that they are going to open a gambling place at one of the mining camps.

'I am going after them. I am still weak, and my shoulder—fortunately it is the left—sometimes hurts me consumedly. It is, of course, still in bandages, but it will take nearly three weeks to Omaha, for the steamer stops at all sorts of wayside stations, so I shall be quite fit by the time I get up there. I have bought three horses, one for my own riding and two to draw a light cart with our provender. The boy will drive it. I am not going to be beaten by this fellow, and sooner or later I will bring him and his accomplice to book, and clear this matter up to the bottom. Don't be uneasy about me; I have had a pretty sharp lesson, and shall not be caught napping again.

'I shall begin to let all the hair grow on my face from the day I leave, and shall have plenty of time to raise a big crop before I meet them again; and as he can have had but a casual look at me there can be no chance of his recognising me, got up in a regular miner's outfit, which I understand to be a dirty red shirt, rough trousers, and high boots. I have written to the Horse

Guards for extension of leave, and, as I told you in my last, shall, if I am pushed for time in the end, make my way across the Pacific to India without returning. Of one thing I am determined. Dorothy Hawtrey shall be completely cleared, even if it takes so long that I have to send my papers in and sell out.

'Of course, when you write, you will merely say that I have gone West, and let it be supposed that I am after buffalo. I will write whenever I get a chance. You might send me a line two or three months after you get this, directed to me, Post Office, Sacramento, telling me how things are going on, and how the Hawtreys are. Say anything you like from me. I do hope they have not heard about my having been hurt.'

In a postscript was added: 'If anyone has stepped into Halliburn's shoes, don't fail to mention it. It will hurt, of course, but I knew my chances were at an end from the moment she found out that I had doubted her.'

'It is a long letter, father,' Dorothy said, as he laid it down beside him and turned to his neglected breakfast.

'Yes, it is rather a long letter,' he said absently.

'Was he badly hurt?' she asked, seeing that he did not seem as if he was going to say more.

'Hurt?' he repeated, as if he had almost forgotten the circumstance, and then, rousing himself, went on: 'Yes, he had a very narrow escape of his life. It seems a man crept up behind him as he was sitting on the wharf, with a bowie, which is a big clasp knife with a blade which fastens by a spring. Fortunately he heard the fellow just in time, and was in the act of rising when he struck him, and the blade fell just behind the shoulder and penetrated its full depth between the shoulder-blade and the ribs. He says he is getting round again nicely; his shoulder is still bandaged, and hurts him sharply at times, but he is going up the river in a steamboat, and will be two or three weeks on board, and he expects to be quite well by the time he lands; then he will be at the edge of what they call the plains.'

Dorothy was silent for some time.

'Was he robbed, father?'

'Only a few dollars; he says he had fortunately emptied his pockets before leaving the hotel.'

'I suppose he is going to hunt out on the plains?'

'Yes, he is going to hunt, Dorothy.'

'What will he hunt, father?'

'I believe there are all sorts of game, dear—buffaloes and deer, and so on.'

'But there are Indians too, father, are there not? I have read about emigrant trains being attacked.'

'Yes, I suppose there are Indians,' Mr. Hawtrey replied vaguely.

'Can't I read the letter, father?' she asked timidly, after another long pause.

'No, I don't think so, my dear. No, it was written to Mr. Danvers, and it was to some extent a breach of confidence his forwarding it to me, but I suppose he thought I ought to see it.'

Dorothy was silent again until her father had finished his breakfast.

'Don't you think I ought to see it too, father?' she repeated. 'Why shouldn't I? If there is anything about me in it, I think I have almost a right to read it. Why should I be kept in the dark? I don't see what there can be about me, but if there is, wouldn't it be fair that I should know it?'

'That is what I have been puzzling myself about, Dorothy, ever since I opened it. I think, myself, you have a right to know. The more so that you have been so hard and unjust on the poor fellow—but I promised him not to say anything about it.'

'But you did not promise him not to show me the letter,' Dorothy said quickly, with the usual feminine perspicacity in discovering a way out of a difficulty short of telling an absolute untruth.

Mr. Hawtrey could not help smiling, though he was feeling deeply anxious and puzzled over what he had best do.

'That is a sophistry I did not think you would be guilty of, Dorothy; though it had already occurred to me. At the time I made the promise I thought his request was not fair to you and was unwise, but the reason he gave was that, having failed here, he did not wish that another failure should be known; and, moreover, he did not wish to raise false hopes when in all probability nothing might come of it. I have been grievously tempted several times to break my promise; I know that Singleton, who also knew, has been on the edge of doing so more than once, especially that day the letter came saying that he was wounded. I will think it over, child. No, I don't see that any good can come of thinking about it. I feel that, as you say, you have a right to know, and as Ned Hampton says it is possible he will go back to India without returning to England, it will be a long time before he can reproach me with a breach of faith. There is the letter, child. You will find me in one of the greenhouses if you want me.'

But as Dorothy did not come out in an hour, Mr. Hawtrey went back to the house and found her, as he expected, in the little room she called her own. She was sitting on a low chair with the letter on her knees; her eyes were red with crying.

'Was I right to show you the letter, child?' he asked, as he sat down beside her.

'Of course you were right, father. I ought to have known it all along,' she said, reproachfully. 'It was right that I should be punished—for I was hard and unjust—but not to be punished so heavily as this. Did he go out from the first only on my affairs, and not to hunt or shoot, as I supposed?'

'He went out only for that purpose, Dorothy. He told me before he started that if he found they had gone out there, he would follow, however long it might take. You must remember that you said yourself that you wished him not to interfere farther in your affairs, and he was anxious, therefore, for that and the other reason I gave you, that you should suppose that he had gone out simply for his own amusement. As I saw no more reason why they should have gone to the United States than on to the Continent, although he thought they had, there was no particular reason why I should not give him the promise he asked; and it was not until the letter came at Chamounix, saying that he had got on their traces, that I had any thought of breaking the promise, although Singleton, who said he had never actually promised, wanted very much to tell you that Ned had not, as you supposed, gone away for amusement, but to unravel that business.'

'It was wrong,' she said decidedly. 'I know it was chiefly my own fault. I might have been vexed at first, but I ought to have known. I ought, at least, to have been able to write to him to tell him that I would not have him running into danger on my account.'

'Your letter would not have reached him had you done so, my dear. There was no saying where to write to him, and he would have left New York before your letter arrived; indeed, he only stayed there three days, as he went down by the first steamer to New Orleans.'

'It would have been a comfort for me to have written, even if he had never got it,' she said. 'Now, he may never hear.'

'We must not look at it in that light, Dorothy,' Mr. Hawtrey said, with an attempt at cheerfulness. 'Ned Hampton has got his head screwed on in the right way, and, as he says, he won't be taken by surprise again. He has been close on these people's heels twice, and I have strong faith that the third time he will be more successful. What he is to do in that case, or how he is to get the truth out of them, is more than I can imagine, and I don't suppose he has given that any thought at present. He must, of course, be guided by circumstances. It may not be so difficult as it seems to us here. Certainly there is no shadow of a chance of his getting them arrested in that wild country, but, as they will know that as well as he does, it might prove all the easier for him to get them to write and sign a confession of their share in the business. There, I hear wheels on the gravel outside; no doubt it is Singleton—he has been over every morning for the last ten days to see if we have news. This will gladden his heart, for he is as anxious about Ned as if he had been his son.'

He was about to take up the letter when Dorothy laid her hand on it.

'Tell him the news, father, please; I want to keep the letter all to myself.'

Mr. Hawtrey went out to meet his friend, who was delighted to hear of Ned Hampton's recovery, but fumed and grumbled terribly when he heard of his plans.

'Upon my word, Hawtrey, I hardly know which is the most perverse, Dorothy or Ned Hampton; they are enough to tire the patience of a saint. Where is the letter?'

'I have given it to Dorothy, and she declines to give it up even for your reading.'

'So that is it. Then he has let the cat out of the bag at last, Hawtrey; that is a comfort anyhow. And how did she take it?'

'She was very much upset—very much; and she says she ought to have known it before.'

'Of course she ought—that is what I said all along; and she would have known if we hadn't been two old fools. Well, give me the contents of the letter as well as you can remember them.'

Mr. Hawtrey repeated the substance of the letter.

'Well, well, we must hope for the best, Hawtrey. He is clear-headed enough, and he will be sharply on his guard when he overtakes them; and he will look so different a figure in a rough dress after that long journey I can hardly think the fellow is likely to recognise him again.'

'Will you come in, Singleton?'

'Not on any account. We had best let Miss Dorothy think the matter out by herself. I fancy things will work out as I wish them yet.'

Dorothy sat for a long time without moving; then she drew a small writing-table up in front of her, and, taking a sheet of note-paper, began to write after a moment's hesitation.

'My dear Captain Armstrong,—When I saw you last I told you that I would let you know should the strange mystery of which I was the victim ever be cleared up. It is not yet entirely cleared up, but it is so to a considerable extent, as the woman who personated me has been traced to America, where she went a week after the robbery, and my portrait has been recognised as her likeness by a number of persons at the hotel where she stopped. This encourages us to hope that some day the whole matter will be completely cleared up. I received this news on the day after you left Chamounix, but I did not write to you before because I wanted to think over what you said to me in quiet.

'I have done so, and I am sorry, very sorry, Captain Armstrong, to say that I am certain my feelings towards you are not, and never will be, such as you desire. I like you, as I told you when you first asked me the question, very, very much, but I do not love you as you should be loved by a wife. I hope we shall always be good friends, and I wish you, with all my heart, the happiness you deserve, though I cannot be to you what you wish. I do not hesitate to sign myself your affectionate friend, Dorothy Hawtrey.'

The note was written without pause or hesitation. It had been thought out before it was begun. It was strange, even to herself, how easily it had come to her, after having had it so much on her mind for the last month. She wondered now how she could have hesitated so long; how she could ever have doubted as to what she would say to him.

'I thank God I did not write before,' she murmured, as she directed the letter. 'I might have ruined my life and his, for, once done, I never could have drawn back again.'

CHAPTER XX

A caravan—consisting of ten waggons, drawn by teams of six, eight, and ten bullocks, five or six lighter vehicles of various descriptions, half-a-dozen horsemen, and a score of men on foot—was making its way across an undulating plain.

Few words were spoken, for what was there to talk of when one day was but a picture of another? The women, sitting for the most part in the waggons, knitted or worked with but an occasional remark to each other. The men, walking with the oxen, kept on their way as doggedly as the animals they drove, and save for the occasional crack of a whip or a shout from one of the men to his beasts, and the occasional creaking of a wheel, the procession might have seemed to an onlooker a mere phantasmagoria of silent shapes. But the sun was getting low and the oxen beginning almost insensibly to quicken their pace, and all knew that the long day's journey was nearly over, and the water-holes could not be far ahead.

Half an hour later these are reached, and at once a babel of sounds succeeds the previous silence. The children of all ages leap joyfully from the waggons, the men loose the oxen from their harness, and then some of them take them to the lowest water-hole, while the rest, and even the women, lend a hand at the work, and arrange the great waggons into the form of a square. As soon as this is done fires are made with the bundles of bush that the boys and girls have cut during the earlier part of the day's journey and piled on the tailboards of the waggons—long experience having taught them that everything that could burn had been long since cut down or grubbed up within a wide radius of the halting-place.

The horses are hobbled and turned out, to pick up what substance they can find in addition to a slice or two of bread that most of their owners have set apart from the over-night baking. Kettles are soon hanging over the fires, and it is not long before most of the women have their dough ready and placed in iron baking-pots over the red-hot embers, a pile of which is raked over the cover so as to bake it evenly right through. Two or three deer had been shot in the morning by the hunters, and the joints hung over the fires give an appetising odour very welcome to those whose chief article of diet for many weeks has been salt meat.

In one corner of the square a group of three or four men are seated round a fire of their own. It is they whose rifles have provided the meat for the camp, and who in return receive a portion of bread from each of the families composing the caravan.

'We shall not get much more hunting,' one of them said; 'we are getting to the most dangerous part of our journey. We have been lucky so far, for though we know that we have been watched, and have seen several parties of Redskins, none of them have been strong enough to venture to attack us. But now that every express rider we have met has warned us that there is trouble here, that strong caravans have been overpowered and the emigrants massacred, there will be no more wandering away far from the camp. You will have to travel the same pace as the rest of us, Ned,' he added, to the bearded figure next to him. 'It beats me how you have got through as you have, without having your hair raised.'

'I have only made extra journeys where, by all accounts, no Indians have been seen about for some time. Besides, it is only about three or four times we have made two journeys in one. We have simply, when the party we were with have made up their minds to stop a day or two at a water-hole to rest their beasts and to wash their clothes, gone on the next morning with another party who had finished their rest. There seem to be regular places where every caravan that arrives makes a halt for a day or so. We have done this seven times, so I reckon that we have gained fourteen days that way and on five days we have made double journeys, so that altogether we have picked up something like nineteen days on the caravan we started with.'

'Your critters are in good condition, too,' the man remarked.

'Yes, I have been fortunate with the hunting. One can always get half a pound of flour for a pound of meat, so that I still have almost as much as I started with, and I always give each of the horses four pounds of bread a day. One cannot expect that horses can be kept in condition when they are working day after day and have to spend their nights in searching for food and then not getting half enough of it.'

'These Indian ponies can do it; no one thinks of feeding a horse on the plains. They have got to rustle for themselves.'

'That may be, but these three horses have not been accustomed to that sort of thing. No doubt they have always been fed when they have worked, and they would soon have broken down under the life that comes natural to the half-wild ponies of the plains. However, it has paid to keep them well; they have come along without halts, and, as you see, they are in as good condition as when they started. In better condition indeed, for they are as hard as nails and fit to do anything.'

'That young mate of yours is a good 'un, and takes wonderful care of the critters. He is British too, I suppose?'

'Oh, yes, we came out together.'

'Ain't no relation of yourn?'

'No. I was coming out and so was he, and we agreed to come together. It is always a good thing to have someone one knows at home with one.'

'That is so,' the man agreed. 'A good mate makes all the difference in life out here. It is easy to see the young 'un thinks a heap of you, and I guess you could reckon on him if you got into a tight corner. He is a tough-looking chap, too. Well, I reckon the meat's done. You had better give a call for your mate. Where has he gone to?'

'He is at the cart,' Ned said, as he stood up and looked round. 'Jacob, supper is ready.'

'I am coming,' was called back; but it was another five minutes before Jacob came up and seated himself by the fire.

'What have you been up to, Jacob?'

'I fetched a couple of buckets of water, and I have been a-giving the cart a wash down and a polish.'

The hunters looked at the lad in surprise.

'Do you mean that?' one asked; and on Jacob nodding they all burst into a hearty laugh.

'Well, I reckon, Jacob, as that's the first cart as ever was washed out on these plains. Why, what is the good of it, lad? What with the mud-holes in the bottoms and the dust where the wind has dried the track, it will be as bad as ever afore you have gone half an hour; besides, who is a-going to see it?'

'I don't care for that,' Jacob said sturdily; 'if it has got to get dirty it has got to; that ain't my fault; but it is my fault if it starts dirty. It ain't often one gets a chance o' doing it, but as we was in good time to-day I thought I would have a clean up. Ned had seen to the horses, so I looked to the cart.'

It had taken Captain Hampton immense trouble to accustom Jacob to call him by his Christian name. He began by pointing out to him that were he to call him 'Captain' or 'sir' it would at once excite comment, and that it was of the greatest importance that they should appear to be travelling together on terms of equality.

'Unless you accustom yourself always to say "Ned" the other words are sure to slip out sometimes. This journey is going to be a hard one, and we have got to share the hardships and the danger and to be comrades to each other, and so you must practise calling me Ned from the time we go on board the steamer.'

It had not been, however, until they had been out on the plains for some time that Jacob had got out of the way of saying 'Captain' occasionally, but he had now fallen into 'Ned,' and the word came naturally to his lips.

'I think the idea is right, Jacob. Absolutely, washing the cart may seem useless. So it is to the cart, but not to you. There is nothing like doing things as they should be done. When one once gets into careless habits they will stick to one. I always give my horse a rub down in the morning and again before I turn it out after it has done its work. I think it is all the better for it, and I like to turn out decently in the morning, not to please other people, but for my own satisfaction.'

'I reckon you are about right,' the oldest of the party said; 'a man who takes care of his beast gets paid for it. You don't have no trouble in the morning. Your three critters come in at once when they hear you whistle. I watched them this morning and saw you give them each a hunch of bread and then set to work to rub them down and brush their coats, and I says to myself, "That is what ought to be between horse and master. If we was attacked by Redskins you and that young chap would be in the saddle, and ready either to fight or to run, afore most of them here had begun to think about it."'

One of the horses in the cart always carried a saddle, and Jacob sometimes rode it postilion fashion, and also rode out with Ned Hampton when the start of the caravan was late and he went out to try to get a shot at game before they moved. In this way he had got to ride fairly, which was Ned's object in accustoming him to sit on horseback, as he told him there was never any saying when it might not be necessary to abandon the cart and to journey on horseback. The two draught horses were ridden in turns, and when the lad rode with his master the third horse was always summoned by a whistle to accompany them, and cantered alongside its companion until both halted, when Ned caught sight of game and went forward alone in its pursuit. Jacob was also taught to use a pistol, and by dint of steady practice had become a fair shot.

The meal was just finished when there was a shout from the man placed on the lookout a hundred yards from the encampment.

'What is it?' a boy posted just outside the waggons shouted back.

A dead silence fell on the camp until, a minute later, they heard the reply, 'It is only the express rider.'

Many of the men rose and moved towards the narrow opening left between two of the waggons to give admittance to the square.

The passage of an express rider was always an event of prime interest. These men were their only links with the world. Often if they met them on the way they would not check the speed of the ponies, but pass on with a wave of the hand and a shout of 'All's well,' or 'Redskins about; keep well together.' It was only when a rider happened to reach one of the pony stations, often forty or fifty miles apart, while the caravan was there, that they could have a talk and learn what news there was to be told of the state of the country ahead. It was uncertain whether the rider would draw rein there; he might stop to snatch a bit of food and a drink before he rode on. This hope grew into certainty as the footsteps of a horse at a gallop were heard approaching. The man threw himself off his pony as he entered the square, and the light of the fire sufficed to show that the horse was in the last state of exhaustion, its chest was flecked with foam, its sides heaved in short sobs, its coat was staring.

'Give it half a bucket of water with half a tumbler of whisky in it,' the man said hoarsely. 'It has saved my life.'

Jacob ran up with half a pail of water, and Captain Hampton emptied the contents of his flask into it.

'Thanks, mate,' the rider said, holding out his hand; 'that is a good turn I won't forget.'

The horse at first refused to drink. Captain Hampton dipped his handkerchief in the bucket and sponged its nostrils and mouth, while its rider patted its neck and spoke encouragingly to it. At the next attempt it sipped a little and then drank up the rest without hesitation.

'It will do now,' its rider said, with a sigh of relief; 'it has carried me eighty miles, and for the last twenty of them I have been hotly chased by the Redskins; they were not a hundred yards behind when at the last rise I caught sight of your fires and knew that I was saved. It was my last chance, for I knew that if I did not find a party at these water holes it was all up with us.'

'Then there are Redskins near,' one of the men asked; 'how many of them?'

'Not above a dozen; it was a big band, but there were not more than that chased me. They won't venture to attack this outfit, but some of you had best turn out with your rifles at once, and get your oxen and horses in. If you don't you are not likely to find them here in the morning.'

This started the whole camp into activity. A waggon at the entrance was turned round so as to give more room to the animals to pass in; the boys were set to work to carry blazing brands and brushwood outside, and to relight the fires, at a distance of thirty or forty yards round the waggons, while the embers of those inside were at once scattered; the children were all placed for safety in the waggons, where Captain Hampton, whose horses had come in at once to his whistle, took his place with four or five other men in readiness to keep the Indians at a distance, if they showed themselves. The rest of the men, armed to the teeth, went out to drive in the animals. This was accomplished without interruption, and the waggon was then moved back into its place, the boys posted on watch all round, and the men gathered round the express rider to hear the news.

'It is mighty bad news, boys,' began the express rider, 'I can tell you—I saw nothing particular wrong till I got near the pony station, though I noticed that a big gang of Redskins had ridden across the track. Directly I fixed my eye on the station I saw as something was wrong. There was the stockade, but I did not see the roof of the station above it. I took a couple of turns round afore I went near it, but everything was still and I guessed the red devils had ridden off, so I made up my mind to ride straight in and take my chance. When I did, I tell you it made me feel a pretty sick man. The hut was down, but that was not the worst of it; there was bodies lying all about; men and women, scalped in course; there was what had been five waggons just burnt up, piles of flour and meat and other things all about, and it was clear that, after taking all they could carry, the Redskins had emptied the barrels, chucked them into the waggons and set them alight.

'It wuz clearly a surprise, for there wer'n't a dead Redskin about. That didn't go for much, cause they would have buried them; but I looked pretty close round and could see nary sign of blood except where the whites were lying. The Redskins had left their ponies at a distance, had scaled the stockades without being noticed, and then had fallen upon them afore they had time to get hold of their arms. There was a dead man at each corner of the stockade; them four had been stabbed or tomahawked, and so no alarm had been given. I counted fifteen dead bodies besides the station-keeper and his mate: they was pretty near all children or oldish women and men. I guess they carried off all the young women and some of the men.'

A deep groan of horror and fury broke from his hearers.

'Ay, it is one of the worst businesses there has been yet,' he said; 'and there has been some bad massacres in this part too. Men says those people up the Salt Lake stirs the Redskins up agin emigrants, but I can't believe as human nature is as bad as that. Well, I did not wait long, you may be sure. I got a bucket and filled it at the station-keeper's bar'l and put half a dozen pounds of flour in from one of the heaps, and stirred it up and give it to the pony. I guessed he would want it afore he had done. Then I rode on quiet, keeping a pretty sharp look out, you bet, till I got half way to this place. Then I got sight of a big lot of Redskins over on the right, and you may bet your boots I rode for it. They came down whooping and yelling, but the crittur is one of the fastest out on the plains, and if he had been fresh I should not have minded them a cent. Most of them soon gave it up, but about a dozen laid themselves out for me, and I tell you I have had to ride all I knew to keep ahead of them. The last half-mile I could feel that the poor beast could not go much further, and if I had found nary waggon here I had made up my mind to lie down at one of these holes and fight it out. I reckon some of them would never have got back to their tribe to tell how my scalp was took.'

Guards were posted round the waggons as soon as the cattle were in and the entrance closed, although, as the express rider said, there was little fear of an attack, as even if the main body of Indians had followed those who pursued him, they would not venture upon such an enterprise, when they would be sure that the emigrants would be watchful and prepared, but would be far more likely to fall upon them on the march. He thought it still more likely that there would be no attack whatever.

'They have got a grist of scalps,' he said, 'and as much booty as they could carry away. They will be making straight back to their villages to have their dances and feasts. You have a good chance of getting on safely now.'

Captain Hampton volunteered to form part of the first watch. The news had rendered him very uneasy. He told Jacob that he might as well come out with him.

'I am troubled about this affair, Jacob,' he said, when they had taken their place, about a hundred yards away from the waggons. 'You know, I was saying to-day that we might possibly overtake them at any time. If they have travelled at the rate at which the heavy trains move they may very well have been with that party who have been massacred by the Indians. Mind, I do not think that they were; I should say that most likely they have gone on as fast— or possibly even faster—than we have. The waggon they brought was a light one, though it was heavier than ours, but they have six horses. Then, as we have heard, sometimes parties all with light waggons and carriages join and travel together, and so get along much faster than ordinary trains. I think they would have pushed on as fast as they possibly could. I feel sure that if they had a hand in that attack upon me, the man who started by the steamer in the morning would find out before he went on board that I had been taken to the hotel, and that I was alive.

'Probably I may have been reported as much worse than I really was, and they would count upon the wound being a mortal one. Still they could not be sure of it, and would decide to push across the plains as rapidly as possible, in case I should recover and pursue them. Still there is just the possibility that feeling confident that I should die they might take it quietly, and have been in that caravan. It seems to render everything uncertain. Before, we knew they were ahead of us, and that sooner or later we should come upon them in California, if we did not overtake them on the journey; now, we know that possibly they have been killed, and the girl carried off by the Indians.'

'But we shall pass by the place to-morrow, Ned, and you will be able to see if they are there.'

'We shall not be able to see that, Jacob; the vultures and wild dogs make very short work of those who fall out here on the plains. When we get there to-morrow we shall find nothing but cleanly-picked bones.'

This turned out to be the case. The caravan camped four miles short of the scene of the massacre, and made a detour in the morning to avoid it. Captain Hampton rode over early with the hunters, but found, as he expected, that the vultures and dogs had done their work. Two days later the train arrived at Salt Lake City. Here were a great number of waggons and emigrants, for most of those crossing the plains made a halt of some duration here, both to rest their animals and to enjoy a period of quiet, undisturbed by fears of the dreaded Indian war whoop. There was, too, an opportunity for trade with the Mormons, from whom they obtained meat, grain, and vegetables, in exchange for tea, sugar, axes, and materials for clothes.

Captain Hampton remained but a night, spending the evening in examining the newly-raised settlement, and wondering at the strange band of ignorant enthusiasts who had thus cut themselves off from the world and forsaken everything in their blind belief in an impostor as ignorant but more astute than themselves. He made many inquiries as to the possibility of getting together a band to follow up the Indians who were the authors of the massacre four days before, in order to punish them and to rescue the captives they might have carried off, but among the Mormons he found nothing but a dull apathy as to anything outside their own colony, while the emigrants were all too much bent upon pressing forward towards the land of gold, to listen to anything that would cause delay. He had mooted the subject to the men of his own party, but they had shaken their heads.

'I doubt whether it is possible, Ned,' one of them said. 'It 'ud need a mighty strong party to venture into the hills after them Redskins. We don't know what tribe they were or where they came from, and they would be a sight more likely to find us and attack us than we to find them. Their villages may be hundreds of miles away. We ain't sure as they carried any women off, though like enough they have. No, it won't do, Ned. We ought to have at least a hundred good men for such a job as that, and there ain't a chance of your getting them. It ain't like as when a border village is attacked and women carried off; then their friends are ready to go out to pay back the Redskins and rescue the women, and men from other villages are ready to join, because what has happened to one to-day may happen to another to-morrow, and so all are concerned in giving the Indians a lesson. But it ain't no one's business here. This crowd are all concerned only in getting on as hard as they can. There ain't one of them but thinks that the delay of a week might lose him a fortune; and though they would fight if the Redskins were to attack them, they have not got any fight in them except for their lives, and even if they were willing to go they would not be no manner of use on an expedition like that you talk about.'

Captain Hampton hardly regretted the failure of his attempt to get up an expedition at Salt Lake City. It would have entailed a great loss of time, and the chances that the woman he was in search of had been in the caravan were slight indeed. The stream of emigration was so great that frequently five or six caravans a day passed along, and as she might be a day or a month ahead of him it was clear that the odds were great indeed against her being in any given one of them. The risk of attack by Indians was henceforth comparatively slight, and Captain Hampton was therefore able to push on at a much higher rate of speed. He would, indeed, have travelled much faster than he did, had it not been for the necessity of stopping for an hour or two with each caravan he overtook, so as to ascertain that the party he was in search of were not with it.

At last they reached the edge of the great plateau of Nevada, where the land, cut up in numerous ravines and valleys, and everywhere thickly wooded, falls rapidly down to the low lands of California. A village consisting principally of liquor stores stood just where the road plunged down through the forest. Here every caravan stopped on its way to gather news as to the diggings at the gold fields. All sorts of rumours had reached them on their Western journey, and it was only now that anything certain could be learned.

The accounts, however, were most conflicting. Captain Hampton learnt that there were scores of diggings, and that fresh ones were being opened every day. He had no interest in the reports of their wealth or in the accounts of great finds, beyond the fact that Truscott was likely to make for one that seemed to offer the greatest advantages.

It would probably be a newly started one, for there he would not find competitors already established. If he really intended to get up a saloon he would almost certainly go down to Sacramento to begin with, to lay in stores and liquors and purchase either a tent or a portable building of some kind; and at any rate somewhat more reliable information than the conflicting rumours current at this station would be obtainable there.

He therefore determined not to turn aside to visit any of the camps, but to go straight down. There was no hurrying until they reached the plains; the horses had to be led every foot of the way. Frequently the road was blocked by long lines of waggons, delayed by a wheel having come off one, or the animals having finally given in. Then there was no moving until scores of hands had chopped down and cleared the trees so as to form a fresh track. In most cases, however, this was unnecessary, as the operation had been so frequently performed that there was a wide belt cleared on either side of the track.

It was with a sensation of deep relief that they at last reached Sacramento. They had learnt on their way down that the place was crowded and that they would do well to encamp just outside its limits. The town itself was indeed but the centre of a city of wood and canvas. Everywhere shanties and stores had been run up, and innumerable waggons served as the abodes of those who had crossed the plains in them. The wharves were a bewildering scene. Craft of various sizes lay alongside, tier beyond tier, discharging their cargoes. The roadway was blocked with teams. Numbers of men were carrying parcels and bales to the neighbouring warehouses. Waggons piled up with goods for the different centres, from which they were distributed by pack animals to distant mining camps, strove in vain to make their way out of the crush. Stores and saloons were alike crowded, the one with anxious emigrants purchasing their outfit for the gold-fields, and the others with miners, rough sunburnt men in red shirts, breeches, and high boots, who had come down to spend their hard-earned gold in a week's spree.

Captain Hampton went from one to another of the hotels, showing the photograph and endeavouring to obtain news, but it was seldom that he could obtain more than a moment's attention from the over-worked and harassed waiters, and in no case was the photograph recognised; he concluded therefore that the party had, like himself, remained in their waggon. After many inquiries, he found that the greater portion of the diggings were either upon the Yuba River, or on creeks among the hills through which it ran. He purchased diggers' outfits for himself and Jacob, together with the necessary picks, shovels, and cradle, laid in a fresh supply of flour, bacon, and groceries, and two days after his arrival at Sacramento he started for the gold diggings.

For a month he journeyed from camp to camp, and then struck off from the Yuba to a spot sixteen miles away, where gold had been first found two months before, and a rush of diggers had taken place, owing to the reports of the richness of gold there. Already the trees on both sides of the slopes above the creek had been cleared, and a town principally composed of huts formed of the boughs of trees had sprung up. Here and there were tents, for the most part of blankets and rugs, three or four rough wooden stores, one or two large tents, and one of framework with sides of planks and a canvas roof. All these had their designations in bright-coloured paint on white canvas affixed to them. After choosing a place for his waggon on the outskirts of the encampment, Captain Hampton left Jacob to picket and feed the horses and light a fire, and then as usual proceeded in the first place to visit the saloons.

He first went to the tents; sat for a time in each of them and chatted with the miners who had just knocked off work and were drinking at the bars. Then he went to the more pretentious building, over which was the name 'Eldorado.' It was evidently the most popular establishment. The tables were all filled with men eating and drinking, while there was quite a crowd before the bar. He strode up there and almost started as he saw between the heads of the men in front of him a girl whom he would, had he met her anywhere else, have taken for Dorothy Hawtrey. For the moment he felt that he was incapable of asking in his ordinary voice for a drink. At last the object of his long search had been gained, and the woman he had followed half across the world was in front of him. He moved away, found a vacant seat at one of the tables, and seated himself there.

A minute or two later a man came up and said briefly, 'Supper?'

He nodded, and a plate of meat was presently placed before him. He ate this mechanically, and then, lighting a pipe, sat listening to the conversation of the miners at the table, one of whom as soon as he finished his meal addressed him with the usual remark:

'Just arrived, I reckon?'

'Yes, I have only just come in. Doing well here?'

'Nothing to grumble at. Where have you been working last?'

'I tried my luck on several places on the Yuba, but could not get a claim worth working.'

'You won't get one here without paying for it, I can tell you; pretty stiff price, too.'

'I reckon to work by the day for a bit, till I have time to look round. I want to see what men are making before I buy in.'

'I reckon you are about right, mate. Men who are in a hurry to get a share of a claim generally get bitten. Besides, before a man with a claim takes a partner in, he likes to know what sort of a chap he is to work with. Didn't I see you come in half an hour ago with a cart with three horses?'

'Yes.'

'Pretty bad road, eh?'

'No road at all; I just followed the line they had cut for the teams of the storekeepers. Though the cart wasn't half full, it was as much as the three horses could do to get along with it.'

'You ain't going to start a store yourself?'

'No, I have a young mate; I work and he makes journeys backwards and forwards to Sacramento; he brings up anything the storekeepers order—flour, bacon, spirits, tea and sugar; it more than pays for the keep of the horses and for our grub, though I never take anything like full loads.'

'You are in luck,' the man said; 'it is the grub that swallows up the earnings. A man wants to find a quarter of an ounce a day to pay his way.'

'How long has this saloon been up?'

'It came five weeks ago—a few days after the others; and they are just taking dust in by handfuls, you bet. Men would come and pay if they didn't get anything for their money but what they can see. That's a daisy, isn't it?'—and he nodded towards the bar. 'We are just proud of her; there ain't such another in the hull diggings.'

'Does she belong to this part of the country, or has she come from the East?'

'She is a Britisher—at least, the old man is, and I suppose his daughter is the same. Well, so long,'—and the miner strode out of the saloon.

CHAPTER XXI

Captain Hampton sat for some time longer watching what was going on. He saw that the girl did not herself serve, but generally superintended the two lads who were serving the drinks, receiving the money and weighing the gold dust that served as currency, a pinch of gold being the price for a glass of liquor of any kind. Two men, one of whom he had recognised at once as being Truscott, looked after the boys attending to the guests at the tables. Now that he obtained a full sight of the girl, he saw that, striking as was the likeness to Dorothy, there were points of difference; her hair was darker, her complexion less clear and brilliant, her expression more serious and far less variable than Dorothy's and lacking the sunshine that was one of the latter's chief charms. Still, he could well understand that one could be mistaken for the other at first sight, especially when dressed precisely alike, and with the face shadowed by a veil. After sitting half an hour longer he returned to the waggon.

'I have found them, Jacob.'

The lad gave an exclamation of satisfaction.

'It is just as I expected,' Captain Hampton went on; 'they have opened a saloon—that large one with the boarded sides. You had better have your supper, Jacob; I took mine in there. I want to think quietly. We have done the first part of our work, but the most difficult is still before us; at least it strikes me it is the most difficult.'

'You will manage it somehow,' Jacob said confidently; for his faith in his master was absolutely unlimited.

Captain Hampton sat for a long time on the stump of a tree smoking and thinking. Now that the search was over, the task that he had set himself seemed more difficult than before. Think as he would he could form no definite plan of action, and concluded that he would have to wait and see how things turned up. He would, he foresaw, have but few opportunities of speaking to the female, and he had already decided that she was a woman with a strong will of her own, and not likely to act upon impulse. Her expression reminded him much more strongly of Dorothy as he had seen her since she had taken offence with him, than of what she was when he first returned to England.

'This girl has had troubles, I have no doubt,' he said, 'and I should say she has borne them alone. Jacob,' he said suddenly, as the boy returned from seeing to the horses, 'I want you to go to that saloon, and take a drink at the bar. Have a good look at the girl there. You said the photograph reminded you of a girl that lived in the court with you. I want you to see if you still notice the resemblance.'

Jacob returned in half-an-hour.

'Well, Jacob?'

'She is like, sir, wonderful like. Of course, she is older and much prettier than Sally was, but she is very like too, and she has got a way of giving her head a shake just as Sally had, to shake her hair off her face. If it wasn't that it doesn't seem as it could be her I should say as it was.'

'I think it is quite possible that it is she, Jacob. Some day you must try to find out, but not at present. We must see how things go on here before we do anything. I shall get work here and you must go backwards and forwards with the team. We must earn our living, you know. I have got money still, but I must keep some in reserve for paying our passage home, or for anything that may turn up; and if we stop here long I shall want to buy a share in a claim. I fancy they are doing well here. There is no reason one should not make the most of one's time. To-morrow you can go to that saloon and say you are going down to Sacramento next day, and would be willing to bring up a light load for them. That may give you an opportunity of speaking to the girl, and her voice may help you to decide whether it is the girl you knew.'

Next morning Captain Hampton went through the diggings; presently he came upon the man he had spoken to the evening before. He was working with two others. He looked up from his work and nodded.

'Taking a look round, mate?'

'Yes.'

'Do you want a job? We are a man short.'

'What are you giving?'

'Five dollars a day.'

Ned Hampton nodded.

'All right,' he said, 'I will come to work to-morrow. Is your claim a good one?'

'We hope it is going to be; we gave a thousand dollars for it. It is well in the middle of the line of the valley, and we reckon it will be rich as we get lower, though at present we are not doing much more than paying our expenses. Do you want to buy a share?'

'I will tell you after a few days,' Ned said. 'What do you want for it?'

'It just depends,' one of the other men said. 'If it is to a man who would do his full share of work we would let him have a quarter for four hundred dollars, for we shall have to do some timbering soon. If it is to a man who is afraid to put his back into it we would not have him at any price.'

'Very well, then, it will suit us both to wait for a week. I will come to work tomorrow on hire.'

'He looks the right sort,' the man said, as Ned Hampton moved away. 'He is a quiet-looking fellow, active and strong. A Britisher, I should say, by his accent.'

After strolling round the camp Hampton looked in at the saloon. There were only three or four men at the bar. The girl was not there.

'I have been round there this morning,' Jacob said when he returned to the waggon. 'I did not see her. They have given me an order for as much as I will carry. They would fill the cart up, but I would not have more than my usual load.'

'You did not know the man by sight at all, I suppose?'

'No. I don't think I ever set eyes on him before.'

'Spirits and groceries, I suppose, principally?'

'Yes; they are expecting flour and bacon up in a waggon that ought to be in to-day.'

'Did they ask you any questions, Jacob?'

'Only if I had been out here long. I said we had been out here a good bit, and had been hauling goods to the camps where we had been. I did not give any time, but it was a long list of camps, and they must have reckoned we had been out here some months. One of them said something about a reference, so as to be sure that I should bring the goods here when I got them, but I said—Reference be blowed. We had been hauling out here long enough, and as we had got a waggon and team it weren't likely we were going to risk them and being shot for the sake of a few pounds' worth of goods: so they did not say anything more about it. I said my mate was going to work here and was going to buy a claim, and that satisfied them a bit. I suppose you are going to have your grub here at one o'clock?'

'Yes. When do you start, Jacob?'

'I will go as soon as we have had dinner. We will get up the tent with the tarpaulin now, if you are ready; then if we go round just after dinner is over in the saloon I will get the orders for the things at Sacramento and be off.'

'I have arranged about working in a claim, Jacob. I will take my meals at the saloon while you are away.'

When they went into the saloon the great bulk of the men were off to their work again, and only two or three were lounging at the bar. Jacob went up to Murdoch, who was setting things straight.

'Have yer got the list ready?' he asked. 'I am just going to hitch up the team.'

'I will get it up for you directly.'

'We will take a drink while you are getting it,' Ned Hampton said. 'I am this lad's mate, and have pretty well arranged about taking a share in a claim, so if you like he can go down regularly for you.'

They strode up to the bar, while Murdoch went through an inner door. He appeared behind the bar directly after with Truscott.

'These are the men that are going down with the cart, Linda,' the latter said to the girl; 'at least the lad is going, the man is going to work on the flat; they want the list.'

'Brandy and champagne are the two things we want most,' she said. 'You had better get eighteen gallons of Bourbon, eighteen of brandy, and twelve dozen of champagne. I have made out the list of the groceries we want. There it is; that comes to thirteen pounds.'

Truscott then made a calculation as to the amount required for the wine and spirits, and drew a cheque on the bank.

'You are sure you think it safe, Murdoch?' he asked in low tones.

'Safe enough,' the other replied. 'They know well enough if they were to take it they would be hunted down; anyhow there is no other way of doing it unless one of us goes down, and neither of us can be spared. We did not reckon on the stuff going so fast, and it would never do to run out. They would go to the other places at once if they could not have liquor here. When do you expect to be back?' he asked, going across to the bar.

'In about four days, if they don't keep me.'

'They won't keep you,' the man said, 'longer than to go to the bank and get the money. To-day is Tuesday; you will get down to the road by to-night and you ought to be there by Thursday afternoon. If you get there in time to load up then and get out of the place you ought to be back by Saturday night.'

'I reckon I shall,' Jacob said; 'that is if all goes right and I don't smash a wheel or an axle.'

'I will give you twenty dollars more than I bargained for if you are back by sundown on Saturday. We shall want the stuff bad by that time.'

Jacob nodded. 'I will do my best,' he said. 'The horses can do it if we don't get blocked with anything. Is there any shopping I can do for you, miss?'

The girl shook her head.

'No, thank you; I have got everything I want.'

'You had better call at the post office when you get to the town,' Ned said. 'If you should think of anything more, miss, there would be time enough if you sent it off in the mail bag to-morrow morning. If you address it, "J. Langley," he will get it.'

The girl glanced at him with some little interest. He had spoken in a rough tone, but she detected a different intonation of the voice to that in which she was generally addressed.

'You are English, are you not?' she asked.

'Yes, miss, I came across from the old country some time ago.'

'I am English too,' she said. 'I suppose the horses and cart belong to you?'

'They are a sort of joint property between us,' he said; 'I work at the diggings and he drives, and I take it he makes more money than I do.'

'What part do you come from?' she asked.

'Mostly London,' he said; 'but I have been working about in a good many places, and I don't look upon one as home more than the other.'

'You are going to work here for a bit?' she asked.

'Yes, it seems from all I hear as good a place as any, and if I can get regular work for the waggon I shall stop here for a while. I am just buying a share in a claim, and I shall anyhow stop to see how it works out.'

'I have not seen you here before,' she said.

'I took my supper here last night,' he said; 'but the place was full. I did not come in in the evening, for I am not given to drink and I have not taken to gambling.'

'Don't,' she said, leaning forward, and speaking earnestly. 'You had as well throw your money away. I hate seeing men come in here and lose all they have worked so hard for for weeks; and then it leads to quarrels. Don't begin it. It is no use telling any one who once has begun that they had better give it up. They don't seem as if they could do it then, but if you have never played don't do so.'

'I don't mean to. I have seen enough of it in other camps. Thank you, miss, all the same for your advice.'

The girl nodded and moved away, and Jacob, having received his list and instructions, presently joined Ned Hampton and they walked away together.

The next morning the latter set to work, and was so well satisfied at the end of two days with the result that he bought a share in the claim. He took his meals at the saloon and went in for an hour every evening. The place was at that time so crowded that he had but few opportunities of exchanging a word with the girl. She generally, however, gave him a nod as he came up to the bar for his glass of liquor. When he had taken it he usually strolled round the tables looking at the play. In the saloon itself it was harmless enough, the miners playing among themselves for small stakes, but in a room at the back of the saloon it was different. Here there was no noisy talk or loud discussion. The men sat or stood round a table at which Monte was being played, the dealer being a professional gambler, whose attire in ordinary clothes, with a diamond stud in his broad shirt front, contrasted strongly with the rough garb of the miners.

No sounds broke the silence here save an occasional muttered oath, an exclamation of triumph, or a call for liquor. It was seldom that an evening passed without a serious quarrel here or at the drinking bar. Twice during the first week of Ned's stay in the camp pistols were drawn. In one case a man was killed, in the other two were seriously wounded.

'I should like to see a law passed by the miners themselves,' Ned Hampton said, as he was talking over the matter with his partners at their work next day, 'forbidding the carrying of pistols under the penalty of being turned out of camp; and it should be added that whoever after the passing of the law drew and fired should be hung.'

'It would be easy enough, pard, to get the law passed by a majority, but the thing would be to get it carried out. There are four or five men in this camp as would clear out the hull crowd. The best part of us hates these rows, and would glad enough be rid of the gang and work peaceably, but what are you to do when you can't have your own way without running a risk, and a mighty big one, of getting shot?'

'Ay, that is it,' another said. 'It would need a sheriff and a big posse to carry it out.'

'Of course, no one man would attempt such a thing,' Ned Hampton said, 'but I believe in some of the camps they have banded together and given the gamblers and the hard characters notice to quit, and have hung up those who refused to go. It is monstrous that two or three hundred men who only want to work peaceably should be terrorised by half-a-dozen ruffians.'

'It ain't right, mate, I allow as it ain't right, but it is hard to see what is to be done. There is Wyoming Bill, for example, who came into the camp last night, cursing and swearing and threatening that he would put a bullet in any man who refused to drink with him. I expect it were after you turned in, mate, but he cleared the saloon of the best part as was there in five minutes. He did not go into the inner room, he knew better'n that; Joe, the gambler, would have put a bullet into him before he could wink; so would Ben Hatcher, and two or three of the others would have tried it. Then he swaggered up to the bar and began to talk loud to the girl there. Some one told them in the inner room and Ben Hatcher and Bluff Harry stept out, pistol in hand, and says Ben, "You had best drop that, Wyoming, and as quick as lightning. It has been settled in this camp as any one as says a bad word in front of that bar will be carried out feet foremost, so don't you try it on, or you will be stuffed with bullets afore you can say knife. I know you and you know me, and there is half a dozen of us, so if you want to carry on you had best carry on outside. I tell you once for all." Wyoming Bill weakened at once, and the thing passed off—but there will be a big muss some night.'

'I should like to turn the whole lot out,' Ned Hampton said, angrily; 'it could not be done in broad daylight without a regular battle, but we might tackle them one by one, taking them separately. Ten men might make this camp habitable.'

'Are you a good shot with the pistol, mate?'

'Yes, I am a good shot, but I don't pretend to be as quick with it as these professional bullies. Yet I have had to deal with awkward customers in my time, and would undertake to deal with these fellows if, as I said, I could get ten men to work with me.'

'Well, there are three of us here besides yourself, and I guess we would all take a hand in the game. What do you say, mates?'

The other two assented.

'We ought to be able to get seven others,' Jack Armitstead, who was the most prominent man of the party, said; 'they must be fellows one could trust; there is Long Ralph and Sam Nicholson and Providence Dick, they are all quiet chaps and could be trusted to hold their tongues. There has been a good deal of grumbling lately; there have been ten men killed here since the camp began, and it is generally allowed as that is too big an average. It is allus so with these new rushes. Chaps as begins to feel as they have made other places too hot for them, in general joins in a new rush. We must be careful who we speak to, for if the fellows got scent of it some of us would be wiped out afore many hours had passed, for if it came to shooting, none of us would have a look in with men like Ben Hatcher or Wyoming Bill.'

'There is no occasion to be in a hurry,' Ned Hampton said; 'we can afford to wait till they get a little worse, but it would be as well to begin about it and get the number ready to act together.'

'You would be ready to act as captain if you were elected?' Jack Armitstead asked.

'Quite ready. I may tell you, though I don't wish it to go farther, that I have been an officer in the British army, and several times been engaged in police duty in a troubled country, where I have had to deal with as hard characters in their way as these men. I have no wish to be captain at all; I am almost a new chum, and many of you have been a year on the gold-fields. I shall be quite willing to serve under any one that may be elected; I have no wish whatever for the command.'

'All right, partner, we will talk it over and fix about who had best be asked. I guess in two or three days we can make up the number. The boys were pretty well riled last night at Wyoming's goings on, and if it hadn't have been that they did not want to make a muss, with that girl in the saloon, I fancy some of them would not have gone without shooting.'

The next evening the saloon was emptier than usual; there were but two or three men at the bar when Ned Hampton, who had finished his supper early, went over to it. The girl herself, contrary to her custom, came across to take his order.

'Good evening, miss,' he said; 'I hear you nearly had trouble here again last night.'

'Very nearly. I cannot think why men here will always pull out pistols; why don't they stand up and fight as they do at home? It is horrible. There have been four men killed in the saloon while we have been here. I thought they would be rough, but I had no idea that it would be like this.'

'It is not a good place for a woman,' Ned Hampton said, bluntly, 'especially for a young and pretty one. Your father ought to know better than to bring you here.'

She shrugged her shoulders.

'It pays,' she said, 'and they are never rude to me.'

She turned away.

A moment later Ned Hampton was tapped on the shoulder, and looking round saw that it was the man who had during the day been pointed out to him as the redoubted Wyoming Bill.

'Stranger,' he said, 'I want you to understand that any one who speaks to that young woman has got to talk with me. I am Wyoming Bill, I am. I have set my mind on her, and it will be safer to tread in a nest of rattlesnakes than to get my dander up.'

Ned Hampton laughed derisively. 'You hulking giant,' he said, 'if you or any one else attempts to dictate to me I will kick him out of the saloon.'

With a howl of fury the man's hand went behind him to his pistol pocket, but quick as he was Ned Hampton was quicker. Stepping back half a pace he struck the man with all his force and weight on the point of the chin, knocking him off his feet on to his back on the floor. An instant later Ned sprang upon him, and twisted the revolver from his grasp; then he seized the half stunned and bewildered man by his neck handkerchief, dragged him to his feet, and thrusting the revolver into his own pocket, shifted his grasp to the back of the man's neck, ran him down the saloon, and when he reached the door gave him a kick that sent him headlong on to his face.

'Now,' he said sternly, as the man, utterly cowed, rose to his feet, 'I warn you if I find you in camp in the morning I will shoot you at sight as I would a dog.'

The man moved off muttering blasphemous threats, but holding his hands to his jaw which had been almost dislocated by the blow, while Ned returned quietly into the saloon, where the miners crowded round him congratulating him on having achieved such a triumph over a notorious bully. Ned was shortly forced to retire, for every one of those present were insisting on his having a drink with them.

On returning to his tent Ned Hampton found that Jacob had just returned from his second journey to Sacramento, and they sat chatting over the events of the trip until it was time to turn in.

'He has gone, Ned,' was Jack Armitstead's greeting when Ned Hampton came down to his work.

'Gone?' he repeated. 'Who has gone? Not Sinclair surely,' for but two of his partners had just arrived.

'Sinclair? No. Wyoming Bill has gone—rode off just at daybreak this morning, with his face tied up in a black handkerchief. They say his jaw is broken. Well, partner, you have done it and no mistake, and the hull camp was talking about nothing else last night. The chaps as was there said they never saw anything like the way you downed him. Why, if this place was made into a township to-morrow, they would elect you mayor or sheriff, or anything else you liked, right away.'

'Oh, it was nothing worth talking about,' Ned said carelessly. 'He was going to draw and I hit out, and as a man's fist goes naturally quicker from his shoulder than the sharpest man can draw his pistol, of course he went down. After that he was half stunned and I expect he didn't feel quite sure that his head wasn't off. A blow on the point of the chin gives a tremendous shaking up to the strongest man. It was not as if he was standing balancing on his feet prepared to meet a blow. I consider it taking an unfair advantage to hit a man like that, but when he is feeling for his pistol there is no choice in the matter. However, it is not worth saying anything more about.' And Ned at once set to at his work.

Nothing further was said on the subject until they stopped for breakfast, when Jack Armitstead said—

'At any rate, Ned, that affair last night has made it easy for us to get the men together for the other job. Those I spoke to and told them you were ready to be our leader just jumped at it, and I could enlist half the camp on the job if I wanted to.'

'Ten will be enough, Jack. It is a matter that must be kept secret, for you must remember that though we might clear out the camp of these fellows without difficulty, we should all be marked men wherever we went if it were known which of us were concerned in the matter.'

'That is true enough,' Sinclair said. 'It would be as much as any of our lives were worth to go into any of the other camps where one or two of these fellows happened to be, if we were known to have been among Judge Lynch's party.'

Ned Hampton went back to breakfast at the cart, as he always did when Jacob was there.

'They have been telling me that you thrashed a man awful yesterday evening,' Jacob began, as he came up. 'I heard some chaps talking about a fight as I was unloading the goods at the back of the saloon, and I wondered what was up, but I never thought as you were in it; you did not say anything about it when we were talking.'

'There was nothing to tell about, Jacob. I knocked down a big bully and turned him out of the saloon; there was no fighting at all, it was just one blow and there was an end of it. I am a pretty good boxer, I think I may say very good; and these fellows, though they are handy enough with pistols, have not the slightest idea of using their fists. The fellow has gone off this morning and we shan't hear any more about it.'

After dinner Ned again went into the saloon. As soon as he approached the bar the girl came across to him.

'Thank you,' she said; 'the men here heard what he said to you, and he well deserved what you gave him. It was very brave of you, as he was armed, and you were not.'

'His arms were not of any use to him, miss, as I did not give him time to use them; besides, bullies of that sort are never formidable when they are faced.'

Ned felt rather doubtful as to his reception by the other desperadoes of the camp; but as soon as the girl turned away two of these came up to him.

'Shake,' one said, holding out his hand; 'you did the right thing last night. It is well for that white-livered cuss that none of us were here at the time, or he would have had a bullet in him, sure. It has been an agreed matter in this 'ere camp, that girl is not to be interfered with by no one, and that if any one cuts in, in a way that ain't fair and right, it should be bad for him. She has come among us, and we are all proud of her, and she has got to be treated like a lady, and Wyoming Bill was worse nor a fool when he spoke as I heard he did to you. He had not been here long and did not know our ways or he would not have done it. We went in and told him last night he'd got to get, or that what you had given him would not be chucks to what would happen if he was not off afore daybreak. Let us liquor.'

This was an invitation that could not be refused, and Ned had to go through the ceremony many times before he could make his retreat. That evening Sinclair and Jack Armitstead came across to Ned's fire.

'We have got ten men, Ned, who are ready to join us in clearing the camp, and we are ready to do it in any way you may tell us.'

'I should give them fair warning,' Ned said; 'there are six of them, including Mason, the gambler, who are at the bottom of all the trouble here. I will write six notices, warning them that unless they leave the camp in twelve hours it will be worse for them. I will write them now, it only wants a few words.'

Each notice was headed by the man's name to whom it was addressed. 'This is to give you notice that if you are found in this camp after sunset to-night you do so at your peril.—Signed, Judge Lynch.'

'Now,' Ned said, when he had written the six papers, 'get six sticks about three feet in length, cut slits at one end and put these papers in them, and then stick them in the ground in front of these men's tents, so that they cannot help seeing them when they turn out in the morning. If they don't take the hint and go we will hold a consultation in the evening as to the steps to be taken.'

The threatened men were all late risers, and the notices were seen by other men going to their work, and the news speedily spread through the camp.

After breakfast Sinclair said to Ned, 'Those fellows have been holding a sort of council together. I saw them standing in a knot before Bluff Harry's tent; I expect by dinner time we shall see what they are going to do. I don't think they will go without a fight. They are all very hard cases, and Bluff Harry and two or three of the others are clear grit down to the boots.'

At twelve o'clock it was seen that the tents of the threatened men had all been taken down and had been erected close together just outside the limits of the camp.

'That means fighting, clear enough,' Jack Armitstead said, when they resumed work. 'I expect they have agreed that one shall be always on watch, and I reckon that the ten of us would not be of much use against them.'

'I quite agree with you, Jack,' Ned said, 'and I have no idea of throwing any life away by an open attack upon them. We must bide our time: for a day or two they will no doubt keep together, but they will soon get careless and then we can act.'

In the evening the men went to the saloon in a body, and standing at the bar indulged in much defiant language of Judge Lynch and his party. So insolent and threatening was their demeanour that the numbers in the saloon rapidly thinned, quiet men soon making their way back to their tents. Ned had not gone there; he thought that after what had happened before, he might be suspected of being concerned in the matter, and that one of the men might pick a quarrel with him. The next day passed off quietly. Ned, on his way back from work in the evening, passed as usual close behind the saloon. As he did so the door was opened and the girl came out.

'I want to speak to you,' she said. 'Those men were at the bar this afternoon. They were talking about the warning they had had, and one of them said he believed that Britisher had something to do with it. The others seemed to think so too. I don't think your life is safe. Pray do not come here at present, and keep away from them—but it would be safer still for you to go to some other place.'

'Thank you for the warning,' Ned said. 'I had not intended to come in for a day or two. They have no grounds for suspecting me more than any one else, but I don't want to get into a quarrel with any of them.'

'They are dangerous men,' she said, 'very dangerous. Pray be careful. It is shameful that things should be like this.'

'We are going to try and make things better,' Ned said, 'but we must wait till they are a little off their guard.'

'Oh, then you are in it. I thought you would be. Yes, it is dreadful. My friends were with them at first, but they see now that they drive people away from the saloon, and they would be glad if the place could be cleared of them. But pray do not run into any danger.'

'I think I can take care of myself pretty well, miss, and I am not alone. I think most of the men here are of the same opinion, and will be glad to see the camp freed of these ruffians.'

'Yes, but not to take a share in doing it. Well, pray be careful. Were anything to happen to you I should know it was because you had punished the man who spoke so insultingly about me. You are not like most of the others; you call me miss, and you try to speak roughly, but I know that it is not natural to you, and that you have been a gentleman.'

'There are a good many in the camp who have been gentlemen,' he said; 'but it makes no matter what we have been, each man has to work for himself here and to keep on the common level, and the master is he who can work hardest and steadiest, or, on the other hand, he who can draw his pistol the quickest.'

'They are calling me,' the girl exclaimed, as she heard her name shouted within. 'I must go now,' and she darted back to the door while Ned walked on carelessly.

'She is certainly marvellously like Dorothy,' he said to himself. 'Her expression was softer this evening than I have seen it before—that makes the likeness all the stronger.'

In the evening Ned heard pistol shots in the direction of the saloon, and a few minutes afterwards Jack Armitstead came up.

'More murder,' he said. 'Ben Hatcher has just shot down two new-comers. They only arrived this afternoon, and knew nothing of what was going on. They walked up to the bar and gave an order. Ben Hatcher was standing there and made some insulting remark to them. They resented it, and he drew and shot them down at once.'

'You had better bring up the other men,' Ned said. 'We will see if we cannot take this fellow as he leaves the saloon to-night. Don't bring them here; the gathering might be noticed; take them forty or fifty yards behind; then I will join you.'

Ten minutes later Ned took a coil of rope and sauntered off to the spot he had indicated, where he was presently joined by the ten men.

'It would be useless trying to take this fellow in his tent to-night,' he said; 'after what has happened they will be certain to keep a good lookout. We must watch as they leave the saloon. Will you, Armitstead, go in there now and seat yourself at a table and see what is going on, and when you see them coming out get out before them, and come and tell us; we shall be gathered just round the corner.'

'I don't expect they will be long,' Armitstead said. 'There won't be much play going on to-night after what has happened. Yes, I will go in.'

There were a few men still sitting at the tables when he entered; they were drinking silently, and watching with scowling faces the group standing at the bar. He took his seat at the table nearest to the door, and in the silence of the place could plainly hear what was being said at the other end.

'I tell you, you were wrong,' Bluff Harry was saying; 'there was no call to draw. The men were new-comers and meant no harm; it is enough to set the whole camp agin us. It ain't no use your scowling at me; I ain't afraid of you and you knows it.'

'Bluff Harry is right, Ben; however, it ain't no use having words ateen friends. We have got to stick together here, and if we does that we can clear this camp out.'

'I don't care a continental what Bluff Harry or any other man thinks,' Ben Hatcher said, sulkily. 'I does as I like, without asking leave from no man; still,

I don't want to quarrel, and as some of you seems to want to make a muss, I will just leave you to yourselves and turn in.' As he turned to leave the bar, Jack Armitstead slipped out through the door and ran round the corner.

'He is coming out by himself,' he said; 'you had best get away from here, for a shout would bring the whole gang upon us.'

Ned led the others down by the side of the saloon, and then out through the tents. They took their station behind one standing on the verge of the camp and waited. In two or three minutes a step was heard approaching. As the man came along, Ned Hampton sprang out and threw himself upon him; the others at once followed, and the man was thrown on to the ground, and in spite of his struggles bound and gagged. Then six of them lifted him on their shoulders, and carried him up into the wood.

The next morning, one of the miners going up to chop some firewood returned with the news that Ben Hatcher was hanging from a tree. Many others ran up to verify the statement. On the breast of the dead man was pinned a paper. 'This man has been tried and found guilty of murder, and has been hung by my orders—Judge Lynch.'

The feeling in camp was one of general satisfaction. The murders of the preceding evening had caused general indignation, and threats had been freely uttered.

Hatcher's companions were among the last to hear what had happened. None of them, on their return a few minutes after him, had thought of looking in his tent; the three whose turn it was had each kept three hours' watch, and had no reason for supposing that anything unusual had occurred. It was not until eight o'clock, that one looking into Ben Hatcher's tent discovered that it was untenanted; the others were soon roused at the news, and Bluff Harry went down into the camp to see if he had gone down on some errand.

'Have you seen Ben Hatcher?' he asked a miner who was cooking breakfast for his mates.

'Ay. I have seen him, and I guess pretty near every one in camp has.'

'Where is he?'

'You will find him up in that wood there, close to that big pine, and it ain't a pleasant sight to look at, I can tell you.'

'Is he dead?'

'I should say so; about as dead as he ever will be.'

Bluff Harry returned to his friends, and they went up in a party to the wood. Hardy as they were, their faces whitened as they looked at the swinging body and read the paper.

Not a word was spoken for a minute or two; then Mason, the gambler, said—

'We had best bury him at once, boys; we can talk it over afterwards.'

Two of the men went down and borrowed picks and shovels. In half-an-hour they returned to their tents, having finished their task. The meal was prepared in silence. When they sat down, Mason said—

'Well, boys, I don't know how you take it, but it seems to me that this is not a healthy place to stop in. We cannot always keep together and always be on our guard, and they may pick us up one after the other. I thought when you were talking yesterday about Judge Lynch that you were away from the mark. He has been to two or three camps where I have been, and it ain't no manner of good bucking against him. My opinion is, the sooner we git the better.'

'I am with you,' Bluff Harry agreed. 'If they came to open fighting I would take a hand to the last, but this secret business don't suit me. I reckon the game is played out here, and we had better vamoose the ranch before the worst comes of it.'

The others were of the same opinion. The little tents were pulled down and their belongings made up into bundles, and before noon each man shouldered his kit and moved quietly off.

CHAPTER XXII

The evening after the departure of the men who had terrorised the camp, a general meeting was held and the proceedings of Judge Lynch were endorsed by a unanimous vote. It was resolved that the camp should be kept free from professional gamblers and hard characters, and Judge Lynch was requested to give warning to any such men as might come, to clear off without delay. Except those absolutely concerned in the affair of the night before, none in camp knew who were the men who had carried it out. It was an understood thing in the mining camps that the identity of Judge Lynch and his band should not be inquired into or even guessed at. Had their identity been established, it would have been unsafe for any of them to have gone beyond the limits of their camp, and the risk would have been so great that it would have been difficult to get men to act, had they not known that the most absolute secrecy would be maintained.

Some of the miners who were in the habit of playing high grumbled somewhat at the expulsion of Mason, who had not himself been concerned in any of the shooting affrays. Two or three of them packed up their kits and left the camp on the day following the expulsion of the gambler and his associates, but the general result was that the saloon was better attended than ever. There was still a good deal of play going on, for cards formed one of the few amusements of the miners, but as long as they played against each other, the stakes were comparatively moderate, and men were pretty sure that if they lost they, at least, lost fairly.

The intimacy between Ned Hampton and the girl who went by the name of Linda increased. She had given him a bright nod the first time he went into the saloon after the revolution.

'You see there was nothing to be nervous about,' he said; 'the matter was very easily carried out.'

'It is a comfort to know that they are all gone. I hope we shall have peace and quiet now. I hope no one knows that you had anything to do with it.'

'No; it is known only to those who took part in it, and no one but yourself knows that I was one of them.'

'No, but some suspect it. My father and Murdoch both do. They were talking about it this morning. They don't know whether to be glad or sorry. Mason paid well for the use of that inner room, but of late custom has fallen off in other respects. During the last two days we have taken twice as much as we were doing before, so that I think things will be about even. They were asking me about you, and if I knew anything of your history; but, of course, I could tell them nothing, because I don't know anything myself.'

'I don't think any of us know much of each other's antecedents,' Ned said. 'For anything you know I may be either an escaped convict or a duke in disguise; for anything I know you may be the daughter of the man you call your father or you may not. You may be a lady of rank, who has, from a spirit of adventure, come out here. You may have been brought up in poverty and misery in some London slum. It is certainly not the rule here in the diggings to ask people who they are or where they come from.'

The girl had turned suddenly pale. She was silent for a moment when he ceased speaking, and then said—

'It is not very civil of you to suggest that I may have been brought up in a slum.'

'I was merely putting it generally,' he said. 'Just as I suggested that I might be an escaped convict for aught you knew.'

Truscott and Murdoch had indeed noticed with some uneasiness that the girl had seemed inclined to be much more friendly with Ned than she had been with any one else since they had come out. On the journey across the plains they had travelled so much faster than the majority that there was no opportunity for forming many intimacies. Since they had been in California they had seen with great satisfaction that she had strictly followed out the line they had impressed upon her, that while civil to all she had treated them with the most absolute impartiality, showing no preference of the slightest kind. The rough compliments paid to her were simply laughed away, and, if persevered in, those who uttered them found that they had no further opportunities of conversation, and that they were completely ignored the next time they came to the bar.

The interests of the two men were so strongly concerned in the matter that they watched her closely, and were not long in noticing that whenever Ned presented himself at the bar she would in a very short time come across from her place behind to speak to him, sometimes only exchanging a word or two, at others, if business happened to be at all slack, chatting with him for some minutes. That day, when as usual they sat down to dinner together, Truscott said:

'You seem to be taken with that young fellow who chucked Wyoming Bill out the other day. I should not encourage him, or it will be noticed by the others, and that will do us harm.'

The girl flushed angrily. 'You can keep your advice to yourself,' she said. 'He is the most decent man I have met out here, and I like to talk to him; he does not pay me compliments or talk nonsense, but just chats to me as he would to any one else. I don't interfere with you, and you had best not interfere with me.'

'Well, you need not be so hot about it,' the man said; 'there was no harm meant.'

And so the subject dropped for the time, but the two men talked it over seriously when they were alone.

Another fortnight passed. Ned worked steadily on the claim, which was turning out exceedingly well. Jacob went backwards and forwards for supplies. The camp increased in size, and most of the miners were doing fairly well. The saloon was crowded at meal times, and in the evening; the back room was still used for play, but no professional gambler had ventured into the camp. Truscott himself, however, frequently took the bank, although always making a protest before doing so, and putting it as a favour. He refused, however, to play for really high stakes, but the amounts staked were considerably above those played for by the miners at the other tables.

Jacob, who occasionally went to the saloon with Ned, was more and more convinced that the woman behind the bar was the girl he had known in Piper's Court; and the sudden change in her face when he had spoken to her as to what her past history might be, had still more brought Ned over to the belief that the lad might be right. He himself was feeling anxious and undecided. He seemed no nearer getting at the end he desired than he had been a month before, and he could not conceal from himself that this girl showed pleasure when she met him, that her manner softened, and that once or twice when he had come suddenly upon her, her cheek had flushed. An occasional rough joke from his mates showed that it was considered in camp a settled thing that he would carry off the woman whose presence was considered by the superstitious miners to have brought luck to themall.

Hitherto, except on the occasions when she came out to speak to him, he had only met her at the bar. She had more than once mentioned that she went out every morning and afternoon for a stroll through the camp while the diggers were all at work, but being unable to arrive at any conclusion as to his best course, he had not availed himself of what seemed to him a half invitation to meet her. At last, however, he determined to see what would come of it, and making some excuse to leave his work soon after breakfast, went up into the camp. From his tent he could see the saloon, and after watching for half-an-hour he saw the girl come out. Marking the way she went, he followed and overtook her just outside the camp. There was no mistaking the look of pleasure in her face.

'Not at work?' she said. 'Is anything the matter?'

'Nothing is the matter, except that I felt unusually lazy, and catching sight of you, I thought if you would let me I would join you. I thought it would be pleasant to have a talk without having that bar between us.'

'I should like a talk very much,' she said, 'but—' and she looked round a little nervously.

'You mean people might talk if they saw us together. Well, there is nothing to talk about. A man and a woman can be good friends just as two men or two women may be—and we are good friends, are we not?'

'Certainly we are,' she said, frankly. Ned's manner had indeed puzzled her; he had always chatted to her as a friend: he had, as she had said, never once paid her a compliment or said a word that might not have been said had there been other men standing beside him at the bar.

'Do you know, when I first saw you,' he said, 'you reminded me so strongly of some one I knew in England that I could have taken you for her?'

'Indeed,' she said, coldly; 'was it some one you knew well?'

'Very well. I had known her from the time when she was a little child.'

'Did you care for her much?'

'Yes, I cared for her a great deal. She was engaged to be married to some one else.'

'Is she married to him now?' she asked.

'No. At least I believe not.'

'Did you come out here to tell me this?' she asked, suddenly facing round upon him.

'Partly,' he replied. 'We are friends, and I thought you ought to know. I am not fool enough, Linda, to suppose that you would be likely in any case to feel anything more than a liking for a rough miner like myself, but I thought that it would, at any rate, be only fair that you should know that much of my past history.'

'Then you still care,' she said, after a pause, 'for this woman who is so like me?'

'Yes, Linda. I shall always care for her.'

'And it was only because I was like her that you liked me?' she said, bitterly.

'No,' he said. 'I do not think the likeness had anything to do with it. I liked you because I saw how well you were playing your part in a most difficult position; how quietly you held your own among the rough spirits here; how much you were respected as well as liked by them. I thought how few young women in your position would have behaved so wisely and discreetly. Of course, you had your father.'

'He is not my father,' she broke in; 'he has brought me up, but he is not my father. We are partners, nothing more. I have a third share in the saloon, and could leave them whenever I chose. There, we have talked enough together: it is just as well that we should not be seen here. It would be thought that we had arranged to meet, and I do not want to be talked about, even if the talk is not true. Good-bye;' and turning she went back into the camp, while Ned Hampton making a wider detour returned to his tent.

That night there was again trouble at the saloon. 'Shooting again, Jacob,' Ned said, as a pistol shot was heard. 'Some quarrel over the cards again, I suppose. I only hope that it was what they call a fair fight, and that there will be no occasion for Judge Lynch to interfere again. However, we may as well go down and see what is the matter.' They went down together to the saloon; a number of men were standing outside talking excitedly.

'What is the matter?' Ned asked, as he arrived.

'Will Garrett, and a man they call Boots, caught the boss there, cheating at cards, and there was a row over it. White drew first, but Boots was too quick for him, and got first shot.'

'Has he killed him?' Ned asked, anxiously.

'They say not, but the boys don't think he will overget it. Those who were there don't blame Boots, for the last two or three evenings there has been a good deal of talk about the play; either the boss had the devil's own luck or he cheated, and several of the boys made up their minds to watch him close. They suspected him three or four times, but he was so quick that they could not swear to it till to-night Boots spotted it, and swore that he saw him cheat. Then there was a tremendous row. The saloon-keeper whipped out a pistol, but Boots had one in his coat pocket and shot from it without taking it out. No one blames him, for if the other had been a little quicker Boots would have been carried out instead of him.'

The men were pouring out from the place now, Murdoch having begged them to leave at once in order that the wounded man might have quiet. One of the miners, who had thrown up his profession as a doctor for the excitement of the gold-fields, had been in the room at the time and was now looking after him. A messenger was just starting on horseback to fetch another surgeon who was practising at Cedar Gulch, thirty miles away. The next day it was known that the surgeons had some hopes of saving the saloon keeper's life. A tent had been erected a short distance from the building, and to this he had been carried and the saloon was again opened. Linda, however, did not appear at the bar, and Murdoch was in sole charge of the arrangements. Ned had called early to ask if there was anything he could do. The girl came to the entrance to the tent. 'There is nothing to be done,' she said, 'the two doctors are both within. Mrs. Johnson is coming over from the store at six o'clock this evening to take my place by him for a few hours. The doctors say it may be a long business. I want to speak to you; if you will come to the back door at half-past six I will come out with you for a short time.'

There was something very constrained and cold about her manner, and Ned wondered what she could want to say to him just at the present time. She came out directly he sent in to say that he was there.

'I do not want to go far,' she said; 'we can walk up and down here and talk as well as anywhere else. Will you give me a plain answer to a question?'

'Certainly I will—to any question.'

'Are you the man who followed us from England, and who arrived at New Orleans the evening before we left it?'

'And was all but murdered that night. Yes, I am the man.'

'Then you are a police spy,' she said in a tone of utter scorn, 'and you have been pretending to be a friend only to entrap us.'

'Not at all,' Ned answered calmly; 'I have nothing to do with the police, nor have I had any desire to entrap you. My name is Hampton; I am a captain in the English army.'

'It is no matter to me who you are,' she said, angrily. 'What is your object in following us here?'

'I might reply by asking what was the object of the two men with you in setting a man on to murder me in New Orleans.'

Her face changed at once. 'I knew nothing of it,' she exclaimed; 'I know we hurried away from our hotel, and they told me afterwards that Warbles had recognised some one he knew on board a steamer that had just come in. But they never could have done that. Were you much hurt?'

'It was a miracle I was not killed,' he said; 'as it was I was laid up for three weeks.'

'I cannot believe that they had anything to do with it. Why do you accuse them?'

'Simply because they were the only persons who had an interest in my death, or, at any rate, in my detention for a period, which as they thought would throw me completely off their track, and enable Warbles, as you call him, to place himself beyond the reach of the law.'

'And you have followed us?'

'Yes, I followed you. I had undertaken the task, and when I once undertake a thing I always carry it through if I can.'

'What was your object?'

'I will tell you frankly. My object at first was to obtain the arrest and extradition of yourself and the man you call Warbles on the charge of being concerned in stealing two diamond tiaras, the property of Gilliat, a jeweller in Bond Street, and of obtaining under false pretences a thousand pounds from a gentleman named Singleton. Failing in doing this it was my intention, if possible, to obtain from you a written acknowledgment of your share in the business. I need hardly say that since I saw you I have altogether abandoned the first intention. I was convinced that you were but an instrument in the hands of others, and only hoped that the time would come when you would undo the harm that had been done by acknowledging that you personated Miss Hawtrey, upon whom the most unjust suspicions have naturally fallen and whose life has been to a great extent ruined by it.'

'Why should it have been?' the girl asked. 'Warbles told me that she could have no difficulty in proving where she was at the time.'

'She had a difficulty. She had been in Bond Street at the same hour, and she could not prove that she was not either in the jeweller's shop or at Mr. Singleton's chambers. Her position has been a terrible one. The man Warbles first prepared the ground by circulating rumours that she was being blackmailed for money, and this gave a reason for her obtaining the jewels. I heard before I left England that in consequence of this cruel suspicion she had broken off her engagement.'

The girl turned fiercely upon him.

'Ah! and you think to go home and clear her and then to receive your reward; and for this you have acted your part with me. Well, sir, I deny altogether any knowledge of what you have been talking about, and I defy you to do your worst.'

She was turning to leave him when he said—'One moment longer. I am in no way acting for myself, but solely for her. My leave is nearly up, and I shall probably return direct to India, in which case I shall not be back in England for another eight or ten years, and she may be married before as many months are passed—may indeed be married now for aught I know. It is for my girl friend that I have been working, not for the woman that I love. You and I are friends now, and were you in difficulty or trouble you could count upon me to do my best for you as I have been doing for her.'

She waved her hand in scornful repudiation of any claim upon him, and went swiftly back to the tent.

'Anything wrong, Captain?' Jacob asked, as he returned to the fire.

'Not worse than might be expected, Jacob. I have spoken to her, told her who I am, and why I came here. Naturally enough, she is sore at present, and considers that I have been deceiving her, which is true enough. At first she denied nothing, but afterwards fired up, and for the present regards me as an enemy; but I believe it will all come right. She is angry now because it seems to her that I have been taking her in for my own purposes, but I think that when she thinks it over calmly she will do what I want.'

Just as Ned Hampton was thinking of turning in for the night a man came up to the fire. He recognised him at once as Murdoch, Truscott's partner in the saloon.

'I have come round to have a bit of a talk with you,' the man said, as he seated himself on a box near the fire. 'Linda has been telling me that you are the man I saw at New Orleans, and that you followed us here. She has also been telling me what you came for, and the girl is downright cut up about it. Up till now I have never known the rights of the job she and Warbles had done in England. She has not told me much about it now, only that she acted the part of another girl and got things in her name, and that the other girl has been suspected of it, and that you want to clear her. Now when I first saw her at New Orleans I took an oath I would do what I could for her, and would see that she was not wronged in any way. I have been watching her pretty close for some time. I could see she liked you. If you had pretended to be fond of her so as to wheedle her into doing what you wanted in this business, and had then chucked her over, I would have thought no more of shooting you than I would of putting my heel on a rattler's head; but I am bound to say that you haven't. I could see that whatever your game was, you were not trying to make her like you; and when I said something about it, when she was talking to me, she flared up and said that you had never been more than civil to her, and there was no thought of love between you.

'I don't think she quite spoke the truth on her side, but that was only natural. Anyhow, I don't feel any grudge against you, and it is only to make things best for her that I have come here. There is nothing hardly I would not do for her, and I want to make things as smooth as possible. You behaved like a man in that affair with Wyoming Bill, and I guess as you are at the head of Judge Lynch's band, and I look upon you as a straight man, and I am not afraid of talking straight to you. It was I who set that nigger on you at New Orleans. I knew nothing about you except that you would have spoilt our plans, and might even get her arrested. Your life was nothing to me one way or another; I had got to stop you and I did it. I told the nigger to hit you so that you would be laid up for a time, but not to kill you; but when I did so I tell you I didn't care the turn of a straw whether he killed you or not. I have been thinking over for the last hour what I had best do, and I concluded to come to you and put it to you straight.

'Warbles is pretty nigh rubbed out; I doubt if he will get round; he takes a lot of liquor every night, and always has done, and that tells against a man's chances when he is hurt. You know well enough that you could do nothing against the girl here. If a sheriff came to arrest her the boys would pretty well tear him to pieces, but the chap that could travel as you have done, from England to the States, and then across to California, would certainly be ready to wait and bide his time, and sooner or later you would catch her.'

'I have no wish to catch her,' Ned Hampton said. 'I have told her so. I believe that she has been deceived throughout by this man Warbles, who is, I know, a very bad lot. I have a strong admiration for her; in person she marvellously resembles a lady to whom I am much attached, and the manner in which she behaves here and remains untouched by the admiration she excites is admirable, and I am convinced that she acted in England solely under Warbles' influence and without any knowledge or thought of the harm she was doing. I am anxious—most anxious—to obtain a written confession from her that would clear the reputation of the lady she impersonated, but if she will not make that confession I shall certainly take no steps whatever against her or put the law in motion to bring about her arrest.'

'That is well spoken, sir, and if I can help you I will. If Warbles dies I shall do my best to be a father to the girl until the time comes when she will choose a husband for herself. I have been a pretty bad man in my time, and in most things she could hardly have a worse guardian, but at any rate I will watch over and keep her from harm, and would shoot down any man who insulted her as I would a dog. That is all I have got to say now. I hope you don't bear any ill will for that job at New Orleans, but I will tell you fairly, I would have done it again here had I thought you were coming to try to win her heart just for your purposes, or you had been scheming to get her arrested and sent to England to be punished.'

'I have got over the affair at New Orleans,' Ned said, 'and feel no malice about it now; and had I done so, the feeling would have been wiped out by the sentiments you express towards Linda. I don't know her real name.'

'Nor do I,' Murdoch said, 'beyond the fact that at first Warbles often called her Sally, I don't know who she is or where he got her from. I know he had her educated, because one day when she was angry she said that she felt no gratitude to him for that, for he had only had her taught for his own purposes. At present he is too bad to talk, but if he gets a bit better I shall try and get the whole story out of him, and if I do you shall have it. As to Linda, she feels pretty bad at present. She has taken a liking to you, you see, and she feels sore about it, but I expect in time she will come round. It depends a great deal on whether Warbles gets well again. She doesn't like him, and she fights with him often enough, but when it is something he's downright set on she always gives way at last. I think she has got an idea that she is bound to do it. I guess it was a sort of agreement when he had her educated that she would work with him and do whatever he bid her. If it had not been for that I believe she would have thrown it up at New Orleans, and for aught I know long before that. If he gets well again she will do as he tells her in this affair of yours. If he dies, you may take it from me that she will own up as you want her to do. You don't mean to hurt her, and I don't think there is any one in England she could go back to, so there can't be any reason why she should not make things straight. Well, I will let you know if there is any change. I shall see you over there, no doubt. She won't be going into the bar, so you can drop in when you like. You are sure to find me there. There is no one else to see about things.'

For the next few days it was understood in the camp that the boss of the Eldorado was likely to get round. It was reported that he was conscious, and was able to talk freely. Indeed, the doctor said it would be much better that he should not talk as much as he did. The doctor had been one of the ten men who had helped to clear out the camp. When not professionally employed he worked at a claim some distance from that of Ned Hampton's party, and as he and his partners messed together instead of taking their meals at either of the saloons Ned seldom saw him. A week after his interview with Murdoch he happened to meet him.

'How is your patient really going on, Ryan?'

The latter shook his head. 'I think he is going downhill fast. He will talk. We have tried opiates as strong as we dare give him, but they don't seem to have any effect, which is often the case with steady drinkers. He has not been a drunkard, I believe, but he has been in the habit of taking a lot of liquor regularly. He scarcely sleeps at all. That girl nurses him with wonderful patience, but she is breaking down under the strain. She wasn't in his tent this morning, and it is the first time that she has been away. When I called the other man, Murdoch, seemed a good deal put out. I don't know what about, and when I told him outside the tent that the other was worrying himself and was a good deal weaker than he was two days ago, he muttered, "The infernal skunk, it is a pity he didn't go down twenty years ago." So I suppose there has been some row between them.'

'He was a bad lot, Ryan; I know something of his past history, and believe that he was a thorough scoundrel.'

'Is that so? I never saw much of him. I don't throw away my money at the bars; my object is to make as much money as will buy me a snug practice in the old country.'

'Quite right, Ryan; it's a pity that more do not have some such object in view, and so lay by their earnings instead of throwing them away in those saloons or in the gambling hells of Sacramento.'

CHAPTER XXIII

The next day it was known in camp that the wounded man was sinking. There was a general feeling of pity for the girl who was believed to be his daughter, but none for the man himself, owing to his having been detected cheating—one of the deepest of crimes in a community where all men gambled more or less.

The next morning it was known that he was dead. He was buried a few hours later. Had he died in good odour, the whole camp would have followed him to his grave; but not one would attend the funeral of a detected cheat, and Murdoch had to hire six men to carry the roughly-made coffin to a cleared spot among the pines that had been set apart as the graveyard of the camp. He himself followed, the only mourner, and those who saw the little procession pass through the camp remarked on Murdoch's stern and frowning face. When the body was consigned to the earth—without prayer or ceremony—Murdoch went down to where Ned was at work.

'Come round this evening,' he said; 'there is a lot to tell you.'

When he went into the saloon in the evening, Murdoch beckoned him into the inner room. Having closed the door, he placed a bottle, a jug of water, and two tumblers upon the table.

'Now,' he said, 'sit down. I have a long story and a bad one to tell you. As I said the other night, I am not a good man, Captain Hampton. I have been mixed up in all sorts of shady transactions on the turf at home, and if I had not made a bolt for it should have got seven years for nobbling a horse. I was among a pretty bad lot at New Orleans, and many a sailor was hocussed and robbed at my place, and I pretty near caused your murder; and yet, I tell you, if I had known what a black-hearted villain that man Warbles—or, as he says his name really is, Truscott—was, I would have shot him rather than have taken his hand. First, will you tell me how much you know of him?'

Ned Hampton told what he knew of the man; of his disappointment at his not obtaining his father's position of steward at Mr. Hawtrey's, of the threats he had made, and how, as it seemed, he carried out those threats by first giving rise to the rumours that Miss Hawtrey was at the mercy of some one who held damaging letters of hers, and then by causing Linda to personate her in the commission of audacious thefts.

'You don't know half of it,' Murdoch said; 'he told it all to her and me, boasting of the vengeance he had taken. You were a boy of eight when Mr.

Hawtrey's wife died—do you remember anything about it?'

'Very little,' Ned replied, after sitting for a minute or two—trying to recall the past. 'I remember there was a great talk about it. She died a week or two after Miss Hawtrey was born. I remember there was a shock, or a loss, or something of that sort, but I do not remember more than that. Oh, yes, I do; I remember there was another baby, and that somehow she and her nurse were drowned.'

'Yes, that was it. Truscott was at the bottom of it; he told us he had been watching for his chance. It seems that when the twins came the mother could not nurse them. Two women were obtained as foster mothers; Truscott got hold of one of them. I believe from what he said she had belonged to the place, but had been away in London and had only returned a month or two, and had had a baby which had died a day or two before Mrs. Hawtrey's were born, and although she had no character they were glad enough to secure her services in the emergency. Truscott, as I said, got hold of her and bribed her heavily to consent to carry out his orders. One evening she pretended to get drunk. She was of course discharged, but being apparently too drunk to be turned out on a wet and wild night, as it happened to be, she was put in a room upstairs and was to be sent away first thing in the morning.

'The two babies slept in cradles in their mother's room. In the morning the one she had nursed was gone and so was the woman. The latter's bonnet was found at the end of the garden which ran down to the Thames. The supposition naturally was that she had awoke half-sobered in the morning, with sense enough to remember how she had disgraced herself, and had determined to drown herself and the child. The river was dragged; the woman's shawl was found caught in a bush dipping into the water, and a torn garment which was recognised as that in which the baby had been put to bed was fished out of the river miles down. The woman's body was never found, but the river was in flood and it might have been swept out to sea in a few hours. A little baby's body was cast ashore below Kew. It could not be identified, but no doubts were entertained that it was the one they were in search of, and it was buried with Mrs. Hawtrey, for whom the excitement and shock had been too much.'

Captain Hampton had listened with growing excitement to the story.

'Then the child was not drowned, and Linda is Dorothy's twin sister! I wonder that a suspicion of the truth never occurred to their father. Had I known all these circumstances you are telling me I am sure I should have suspected it. I was convinced by this scoundrel's manner, when he had an altercation with Mr. Hawtrey at Epsom and threatened him, that he had already done him some serious injury, though Mr. Hawtrey, when I spoke to him, declared he was not conscious that he had suffered in any way at his hands, unless two or three rick-burnings had been his work.

'Certainly, no thought that he could have had any hand in the catastrophe that caused the death of his wife had ever occurred to him. Had I known that the body of the infant had never been really identified, or that of its nurse found, I should have suspected the truth as soon as I found that Truscott and Dorothy's double were acting together. What an infamous scoundrel, and what a life for the girl. But he never could have foreseen that the two sisters would grow up so alike.

'No. He told the poor girl what his intentions had been. The woman who stole her died when the child was four years old, and he then placed her with a woman whom he had known as a barmaid. She was not only given to drink, but was mixed up with thieves and coiners. His expectation was that the girl so placed would necessarily grow up a young thief, and go to the bad in every way; and the vengeance to which he had looked forward was that Mr. Hawtrey should at last be informed that this degraded creature was his daughter. He had the declaration of the woman who stole her signed by herself in presence of three witnesses. Of course it made no allusion to his agency in the affair, but described it as simply an act of revenge on her part. He intended to testify only to the fact that he had known this woman, and at her death had taken the child she had left behind her and placed it with another woman as an act of pure charity. Of course, the part he had played in the matter would have been suspected—indeed, he would have lost half his pleasure had it not been so—but there would have been no proof against him.'

'It is a horrible business,' Ned Hampton said; 'a fiendish business, and he had no real ground for any hostility against Mr. Hawtrey. He would have had the appointment his father had held had it not been for his own misconduct. His own father, on his deathbed, implored Mr. Hawtrey not to appoint his son, as he would certainly bring disgrace upon his name.'

'Truscott represented that he had been scandalously treated and his life ruined by Hawtrey. I have no doubt the matter really was as you say, but he had certainly persuaded himself that he was a terribly ill-used man, and spoke with exultation over the revenge he had taken. It was about four years ago that on his going to see the girl in the court in which he had placed her—'

'It was Piper's Court, at Chelsea.'

'Why, how on earth did you know that?'

'I have a lad with me who was brought up in that very court, and who recognised her as soon as he saw her here; in fact he had remarked on the likeness directly he saw a photograph of her sister.'

'Well, when Truscott noticed the likeness he saw that properly worked there was money to be made out of it, so he took her from the woman she had been with and put her with one who had been a governess, but who had come to grief somehow and was nearly starving. This woman was to educate her, but was to teach her nothing that could interfere with his plans for her. I mean nothing of religion or what was right or wrong, or anything of that sort. When he sent her to the woman, the girl had promised she would do whatever he wanted her to do if he would have her educated. So, when the time came, she was perfectly ready to carry out his scheme. She watched Miss Hawtrey come out from her house several times, noted the dress she wore, and had one made precisely similar in every respect, and, as you know, carried out her part perfectly.'

'Her hair is, as you see, rather darker than her sister's, but she faked it up to the right shade, and the make-up was so good that not only the shopmen but this Mr. Singleton, whom Truscott knew was her sister's godfather and a most intimate friend, was also taken in. I tell you, sir, if you had heard the devilish satisfaction with which that scoundrel went over this story again and again, you would have felt, as I did, a longing to throw yourself upon him and strangle him. I must tell you that Sally had no idea whatever that the girl she represented would be seriously suspected of having carried out these thefts. She knew nothing of Truscott's enmity to Hawtrey. He had told her only that he knew a young lady to whom she bore such a remarkable likeness that it would be easy to personate her. Sally herself had suggested that the girl might be suspected, but he had laughed at the idea and said she could have no difficulty whatever in showing where she was at the time that Sally called at the jeweller's and Singleton's. Sally herself is fond, as is natural enough in a girl as good-looking as she is, of handsome clothes, and that visit to the shop where she laid in a stock of fine clothes was, she admits, her own suggestion. She has kept her room since Truscott's death. She did not say a word as he was telling her his story, but she went as white as death, and got up with a sort of sob when he finished and went out of the tent without saying a word, and has not come out of her room since.

'I saw her after his death this morning, and it cut me to the heart. She was sitting on her bed, and I think she had been sitting there ever since she went into her room, twenty-four hours before. She talked it over with me in a strange hopeless sort of voice, as if the girl who had been brought up in that court in Chelsea had been somebody else. I brought her in some tea with some brandy in it, and made her drink it; and she took it just like a little child might. This afternoon I saw the doctor and told him what sort of a state she was in, and he gave me a sleeping mixture which I got her to take, and I peeped in just now and saw that she was lying asleep on her bed, and I hope she will be better to-morrow. It has been an awful shock for her.'

'Terrible,' Ned Hampton agreed. 'I could hardly imagine a more dreadful story for a woman to hear. She is indeed deeply to be pitied. What are you thinking of doing?'

'I am not thinking anything about it yet. I suppose she will go back to England. As for me, I expect I shall carry on this place. We have been doing first-rate since we came here three months ago. Of course it won't be the same when she has gone. We three were equal partners in it, but I am sure we shall have no trouble in arranging about that. I don't know what I shall do without her; you will hardly believe me, but the eight or nine months we have been together I have got to love that girl just as if she had been my daughter. You see I always doubted that Truscott meant fair by her. Of course, he would have used her as long as she was useful to him, but he would have thrown her off in a minute if it had suited him. She knew I meant fair by her, and when we happened to be alone together she talked to me quite different to what she did to him. It seemed to me that with him she always had in her mind that it was a bargain which she was carrying out. She regarded him as her master in a sort of way, but I do really think she looked on me as a friend. She would not have stayed with us long. At New Orleans she got a partnership deed drawn out. She would not move without it, and one of the conditions she insisted on was that she could leave us when she liked, and if Truscott had pressed her to do anything, such as marry a man she did not fancy, or anything of that sort, she would have chucked it up at once. But she has got lots of spirit and pluck, and though, of course, she is awfully cut up at present, she will get over it before long, and she particularly begged you would not write to England about all this till she has seen you.'

'That I certainly will not do. I don't know that I shall write at all. My idea at present is that it will be better for me to take her home, and then to tell them the story gradually before introducing her to them. I intended going down to San Francisco and taking passage direct to India, but I must give up that idea now. It is clear that she cannot go by herself, and that I must hand her over to her father.'

It was not until four days later that Ned heard from Murdoch that Linda, as they still called her, would see him next morning. On going in he was struck with the change that a week had made. She was paler and thinner, there were dark circles round her eyes and a certain air of timidity had taken the place of the somewhat hard expression of self-reliance that had before characterised her.

'You have heard all the story, Captain Hampton,' she said, 'and I don't know that there would be any use going over it again. I have written out a confession of the part I played under the direction of that man, and I will sign it in the presence of a magistrate and anyone else you like. I thank you for the kindness and consideration that you have shown for me, and hope—I do hope with all my heart—that when you go back you will get the reward for the sacrifices you have made for Miss Hawtrey. I don't think that there is anything else to say.'

'I think there is a good deal to say,' he replied quietly. 'We have to arrange when it will suit you to leave this. I should propose that we go down to San Francisco and take the steamer to Panama and go straight home from there.'

'I have no home,' she said, 'except this. I have no idea of returning to England. I have thought it all over,' she went on, seeing that he was about to speak, 'and am sure that it is much the best for everyone. You know what I have been—a child brought up in the slums, a little thief, a passer of base coins; since then an adventuress and a thief on a larger scale; last a barmaid. Do you think I would go back and take up a position as a gentleman's daughter and mix with decent people? I should be miserable. I should know myself to be an impostor. I should feel that if those I met knew what I really am they would shrink from me with horror. I cannot imagine a more wretched existence. My father might tolerate me, but he could not love me. I should cast a shadow on his life; it would never do. This morning I had a long talk with Murdoch. He has behaved as a true friend to me ever since we met; he has always been good to me, and stood between me and the other. He is ready now to make a sacrifice for me. He will dispose of this business—he has already received more than one good offer for it—and will buy a farm down in the fruit district. I did not ask him to do this; I was quite willing to have gone down to Sacramento or San Francisco, and to have taken a situation in a shop or an hotel, but he proposed the other plan and I have gratefully accepted his offer. There is another thing; I have some money. The other got fifteen hundred pounds for the jewels I stole, and there was a thousand pounds that I got from Mr. Singleton. Mr. Singleton's money we put into the business and Murdoch another five hundred, the rest of that went on our journey and in getting and fitting up the saloon. In the three months we have been here we have earned just that money from the takings in the saloon and the money he won in gambling. Of this our share is a thousand, so that I have now the two thousand five hundred which we got from my thefts. This I will hand over to you to pay the people I robbed. We shall still have enough to carry out our plans; Murdoch has his share of the three months' profits, and we have been offered two thousand pounds for the saloon and business, so you need feel no uneasiness about that.'

'But your father will never permit it, Miss Hawtrey. I am sure that if you will not go home with me he will himself come out to fetch you.'

'It would be useless if he did so,' she said quietly; 'my mind is quite made up on that point; but I have a prayer to make to you. I implore you never to tell him the truth; let him to the end of his life believe that his little baby died as he believed, and lies by its mother. That old grief is past and over long ago. It was but a babe a few days old, and another was left him who has been all his heart could wish. What comfort or happiness could he derive by knowing this story—by learning that his child grew up a gutter girl, a little thief, an adventuress, a swindler? What could I ever do to repay him for this grief and disgrace? In my confession I have said no word of this, nor is it necessary for your explanations; you can tell how you met me here, how we got to be friends, how that man was killed, and how, deeply regretting the past, I wrote the confession of my crime, and you can add that I am resolved that henceforth my life shall be a different one, and that I am looking forward to a quiet and happy life under the protection of a true friend. Surely this will be best for us all—best for my father, best for Dorothy, best for me. You may tell her all some day, if you ever win her, as I am sure you will if she is free on your return. Little did I think when I saw and studied her walk and manner that she was my sister. Perhaps some day in the far distant she will come to think kindly of the girl who was what circumstances made her, and who had so little chance of growing up like herself, and she may even come to write a line to me to tell me so.'

'Here is her portrait,' Ned said, taking it from his pocket. 'As to what you ask me, I must think it over before I can promise you.'

'It is very like me,' she said, examining the portrait, 'and yet it's quite unlike. I wonder anyone could have taken me for her. The expression is so different. I felt that when I saw her, and I put on a veil, for I knew that I could not look bright, and frank, and happy as she did. Think it over, Captain Hampton. I am sure you will see that it is best. What possible good could it be for my father to know all this? If I had been stolen from him when I had been older, and he had come to love me, it would be different. As it is, the truth could only cause him unhappiness.'

Ned Hampton went back to his claim. It had turned out well, and it was growing richer every foot they went down, and had all along been averaging two and a half to three ounces for each of the partners. When therefore Ned said that he had received news that made him anxious to leave, his mates were perfectly willing to buy his share. They had great expectations of the results that it would yield when they neared the bed rock, and they at once offered him a hundred ounces for his share, an offer which he accepted. He had already laid by an equal sum, and after paying his passage and that of Jacob to

England or India, would have recouped himself for all the expenses of his expedition, and he would have some three or four hundred pounds in hand after the sale of the horses and waggon.

At dinner time he received a cheque on the bank of Sacramento, in which his partners had deposited their earnings. Jacob was away and he took a long walk down the valley thinking over the girl's proposal. He acknowledged to himself there was much truth in what she said. It would be a heavy blow to Mr. Hawtrey to find that his daughter was alive and had been so brought up. He would blame himself for having accepted the fact of her death, when by setting on foot inquiries he might possibly have discovered the fraud and have rescued her from the fate that had befallen her. The discovery would certainly not add to his happiness; on the contrary, he would deem himself bound to endeavour to induce her to return to England, and Hampton was sure he would fail in doing so. He acknowledged to himself that his sole objection to the plan was that he himself would to some extent be acting a deceitful part in keeping Mr. Hawtrey in the dark. Certainly he would not be required to tell an absolute untruth, for as Mr. Hawtrey would not entertain the slightest suspicion of the real facts, he would ask no questions that would be difficult to answer. The next day he told Linda that he would act as she wished.

'I felt sure you would do so,' she said; 'it is so much the best way, and you cannot tell what a load it is off my mind. Murdoch and I have been talking over the future. He understands that I want to be quite different to what I have been, and he says I may get a clergyman to teach me the things I never learnt, and we will go to church together; I have never been inside a church. I am sure we shall be very happy. He seems as pleased about it as I am. You must always remember, Captain Hampton, that though I have been very bad, I did not know it was wrong, except that I might be put in prison for it. I think I have always tried to do what seemed to be right in a sort of way, only I did not know what really was right.'

'I feel sure you have, Linda; I do not blame you for the past, nor do I think that anyone who knew all the circumstances would do so.'

'Have you heard from England lately?'

'No, I have not heard since I left. Letters have no doubt been sent to places in the East, where I said I might call for them. When I arrived here I wrote to a friend, and according to my calculations I may get his answer any day. I have been hoping for a letter for some little time. Jacob has called at the post office at Sacramento the last three times he has been down there. I am very anxious to hear, and yet you will understand I am half afraid of the news the letter will bring me.'

'I don't think you can have bad news in that way, Ned,' she said. 'I may call you Ned again now, mayn't I? If Dorothy's face does not belie her she can't be likely to get engaged to another man so soon after breaking off her engagement with that lord. Does she know you care for her?'

'No,' he said. 'I don't suppose she ever will. As I told you, we did not part very good friends. She did not forgive me for having doubted her. I think she was perfectly right. I ought never to have doubted her, however much appearances might have been against her.'

'I think it was perfectly natural,' she said indignantly; 'if I could deceive Mr. Singleton, and be talking to him for a quarter of an hour without his suspecting me, it was quite natural that you, who only had a glimpse of me, should have been mistaken.'

'That is true enough,' he said gravely. 'It was natural that I should be mistaken as to her identity, but I ought to have known that, even though it was her, she could not have been, as I supposed, trying to prevent the exposure of some act of folly, when she had over and over again declared she knew nothing whatever of the matter. I was in fact crediting her with being a determined liar, as well as having been mixed up in some foolish business, and it is only right I should be punished for it.'

'If I loved a man,' Linda said stoutly, 'I should forgive him easily enough, even if he had thought I told a lie.'

'Possibly, Linda; but then, you see, though Dorothy and I were great friends, I have no reason in the world to suppose that she did love me, and indeed, at the time she was engaged to be married to some one else.'

Linda shook her head, quite uninfluenced by this argument. She herself had been very near loving Ned Hampton, and she felt convinced that this sister, whom she knew so little about, must be sure to do so likewise, especially when she came to know how much he had done for her.

Captain Hampton smiled.

'You forget, Linda, that your sister is a belle in society; that she had several offers before she accepted Lord Halliburn, and is likely to have had some since. I am a very unimportant personage in her world. In fact, my chances would have been less than nothing if it had not been for my having been so much with her while she was a child, and being a sort of chum of hers, though I was so much older.' There was a movement as of weights being carried into the place, and he broke off. 'I fancy that is Jacob back with the cart. Perhaps he has got a letter for me. Any letters, Jacob?'

'Three of them.'

One was in the handwriting of Danvers, another was in a male handwriting unknown, the other in a female hand which he recognised at once, having received several short notes of invitation and appointment from the writer. With an exclamation of surprise he hurried off to his tent and there opened it. It contained but a few words—

> 'My dear Ned,—It was very wrong and wicked of you to go away as you did and keep me in the dark. I have read the postscript of your letter to Mr. Danvers. Come back home at once if you wish to obtain the forgiveness of
>
> DOROTHY HAWTREY.'

He read it through twice, then his thoughts went back to the letter he had written to Danvers from New Orleans, and as he recalled the postscript he had added, he felt his face flush like a girl's under its tan. He read through the letter again and again, and with an exclamation of deep thankfulness put it and the other letters in his pocket, took up the hat he had thrown down as he entered, and started for a rapid walk up the hill, too excited to remain quiet, and fearing to have the current of his thoughts disturbed even by the entry of Jacob. It was two hours before he returned. He went first to the saloon.

'Would you ask Miss Hawtrey if I can speak to her for a minute, Murdoch?'

'Of course I will. Have you got any good news? You look as if you had.'

'The best I could get. It is about her sister.'

Murdoch nodded pleasantly. 'Everything seems to be turning out well. Linda and I are going to settle down to a quiet life till the right man comes for her, and now you have good news from her sister; this place seems lucky for us all.'

He tapped at Linda's door. 'Captain Hampton wishes to speak to you for a moment.'

The girl came out at once.

'Your letters are good?'

'They are indeed, Linda. Dorothy has written for me to go home to her.'

'I am glad,' she said heartily, holding out her hand to him. 'It would have been a real grief to me, if after all you have done for Dorothy it had not been so. It will be very pleasant to think of you as not only my friend but my brother-in-law, and, as I have seen Dorothy, to be able to picture you in my mind as happy together. Since you were here we have arranged with the store-keeper who has bought the business that he shall take possession to-morrow, and we shall be ready to start in the afternoon if it will suit you to take us down in your waggon.'

'Certainly; nothing could suit me better. You have not been long in making your arrangements.'

'It does not take long in these parts,' Murdoch said; 'we have just signed a receipt for five hundred ounces of gold, being payment for the Eldorado Saloon, its contents and good-will. It was just as simple a matter as for you to sell your share of a claim.'

Jacob was surprised and delighted when, on his master's return, he heard that he had completely achieved the object of their journey, and that Murdoch and Linda were going down with him the next day to Sacramento to have her confession sworn to before a magistrate, and that they should then return at once to England.

'That is first-rate, Captain. I need not go on calling you Ned no longer, which is a thing I never liked, as being disrespectful and altogether wrong. You will keep me with you when you get back, won't you, Captain?'

'Certainly I will, Jacob; as long as I live and you like to stay with me you shall do so; but I must try to get you educated and find a better berth for you than being my servant.'

'I don't want a better berth,' the lad said indignantly; 'I would not be made a harch-bishop, not if they went down on their bended knees to ask me to take the job—not if I could stay with you.'

'Well, I don't suppose you will be tempted that way, Jacob. At any rate, lad, my home will be yours as long as you like to stay with me. We have been friends rather than master and servant ever since we left New Orleans. You nearly lost your life in trying to save mine there, and have all along proved yourself a good and faithful fellow. Now when we have had supper you had better go for a stroll through the camp; I have got two letters to read.'

Danvers' letter, which he first opened, contained nothing of any very great interest. He had seen Mr. Hawtrey, who had only been up in town for a few days, their house having been let for the season, as Mr. Hawtrey told him his daughter, who had been a good deal shaken by an unpleasant adventure they had in Switzerland in the autumn, preferred remaining quietly at home. 'This seems to be altogether in your favour, old fellow. I had heard of the adventure, in which she and two other girls had a narrow escape for their lives. Halliburn was there at the time, and was one of the rescuing party. I saw the particulars copied from a Swiss newspaper, and I was afraid at first that affair might come on again; but it seems he left next day, and there has been no talk about it since, and this staying down in the country instead of coming up for the season quite seems to put a stopper on that. Hawtrey has paid Gilliat for the diamonds. I hope your quest will turn out successful, and that now that you have run them to earth you will get her to confess; though I don't see exactly how you are going to set about it. I shall look anxiously for your next letter.'

The other letter was from Mr. Singleton; it was not a long one. It began, 'My dear Ned,—I write to tell you that Hawtrey has very properly so far disregarded your instructions that, though he kept his promise to the letter by saying nothing, he yielded to Dorothy's insistence and allowed her to read your letter to Danvers, which the latter had forwarded to him. If he had not done so I should have told her all about it myself. I considered all along that you had acted like a young fool, and I should have done what I thought best for you. As it was I can tell you that mischief very nearly came of our holding our tongues. However, things are put straight now; and though Dorothy does not say much I am sure she has been fretting ever since she heard of that affair at New Orleans. My advice to you is to come home at once. Of course, if you have arranged this affair all the better, but I don't anticipate that you will succeed in that. When you get back Hawtrey will write to her and offer her a round sum and a promise that no steps shall ever be taken in the matter if she will sign a confession. You had better get the name and address of some solicitor at Sacramento, to act as Hawtrey's agent in the matter. I have told Dorothy that I am going to write to you, and asked if she had any message to send. She said she had not, but she laughed and coloured, and I should not be at all surprised if you get a note from the young woman at the same time that you receive this. I know she heartily regrets her folly before you went away. I must tell you, my dear boy, that I have made some pecuniary arrangements regarding you; and that if Dorothy is willing to take you, you will meet with no objection on the part of her father.'

There was no necessity to write, for Ned Hampton travelled to England as fast as his letter would have done. He telegraphed his arrival as soon as he landed and followed his message immediately. Ned Hampton always said that his wife married him without his even proposing to her. No proposal indeed was necessary; the matter was settled the moment he went into the room where she was awaiting him, and she ran into his arms without a word. It was not until they were at dinner that the object of Ned's long absence was alluded to. Then, when the servants had left the room, he said, 'I have brought home an engagement present for you, Dorothy,' and he handed her Linda's confession.

Mr. Hawtrey never knew the truth as to the person who had played the part of Dorothy's double, and, contented with his daughter being completely cleared, asked no questions concerning her. Dorothy, however, was much more curious, and was with difficulty put off until she became Mrs. Hampton. She was very pitiful over the story when it was told to her.

'Oh, Ned,' she cried, 'how dreadful; and it might just as well have been I who was carried away and brought up in that misery. Of course, she was not to be blamed. How could she have been different? It is wonderful she should have been as nice as you say she was. Of course, I shall write her a long letter. I don't know about keeping it from father; but perhaps it is best, as she was such a little baby when he lost her, and it would be an awful grief to him to think how she suffered.'

Dorothy wrote very frequently, and letters came back telling of Linda's quiet, happy life; but Dorothy was not fully contented until three years later she learned that her sister had married a thriving young settler on a neighbouring farm, and that there was every prospect that the trials and troubles of her early life would be atoned for by happiness in the future.

The year after Dorothy's marriage she was delighted to hear from Ada Fortescue that she had become engaged to Captain Armstrong, and she and Ned went up to town specially to be present at the wedding.

Years afterwards the sisters met, for after Mr. Hawtrey's death nothing would satisfy Dorothy but a voyage across the Atlantic, and a journey by the newly constructed line to California. The likeness between the sisters had increased, for the hard look in Linda's face had died away, and had been succeeded by one of quiet happiness, and Captain Hampton declared that he should hardly know them apart, and that Linda was now indeed *Dorothy's Double*.

THE END.

Lightning Source UK Ltd.
Milton Keynes UK
UKHW011946260722
406426UK00002B/32